Citadel of Seven Swords

Skarde: The Wandering Sword

Erik Waag

This book would not have been possible without invaluable help from:

Daniel P. Riley, Editor. https://www.whimsyland.org/

Dr. John T Parce, Beta Reader. https://johnparce.substack.com/

Krzysztof Porchowski Jr, Cover Art. https://www.artstation.com/krzysztofporchowski

Waag Books

Please visit me at Waagbooks.com or @WaagBooks on Twitter

Copyright © Erik Waag 2023

All rights reserved.

No part of this publication may be reproduced, distributed, or transmitted in any form or by any means, including photocopying, recording, or other electronic or mechanical methods, without the prior written permission of the publisher, except as permitted by U.S. copyright law. For permission requests, contact Erik Waag at erikwaag.books@gmail.com.

The story, all names, characters, and incidents portrayed in this production are fictitious. No identification with actual persons (living or deceased), places, buildings, and products is intended or should be inferred.

ISBN: 9798850080617

Contents

1. Chapter One   1
2. Chapter Two   12
3. Chapter Three   24
4. Chapter Four   36
5. Chapter Five   48
6. Chapter Six   67
7. Chapter Seven   82
8. Chapter Eight   99
9. Chapter Nine   114
10. Chapter Ten   131
11. Chapter Eleven   144
12. Chapter Twelve   160
13. Chapter Thirteen   175
14. Chapter Fourteen   187
15. Chapter Fifteen   204

16. Chapter Sixteen	219
17. Chapter Seventeen	229
About the Author	245
Other Works by Erik Waag	246
A Humble Request	247

Chapter One

The trireme slid over the skin of the ocean like a knife across flesh. A massive, straw-headed man pulled at an oar with shackled hands. The man beside him struggled to grasp the oar and keep pace to the beat of a drum. His head dipped low, his breath ragged. The muscular giant guessed the man had a broken rib or two.

"Keep up, fool," he said, his eyes incongruously benign set in his wolfish face. "These bastards will fling you overboard if they think you are of no use."

The injured man had not spoken yet. The mood under the deck of the slaver's ship was grim despite the bright lances of sunlight stabbing in through the wide oar ports. The man glanced at the giant with tired eyes and spoke with a voice like dry reeds, "I fear you are right, Northerner. I am Marus. What are you called?"

"Skarde," the giant said. "Just keep your hands light on the oar."

Skarde could keep pace alone. He pulled the oar with twice the power of any of the hundred or so sweaty-backed slaves. The stock of the men rowing was varied. Skarde had time to study them one by one, even those behind him as short breaks allowed. Most were men of the southern shores, but many, like Skarde, bore the posture, build, and scars of fighting men.

Hour after hour they threshed at the waves. Skarde's calloused hands ached, although he was no stranger to the labors of the sea. Marus fell back into silence as the sun's shafts bent long and grew dim. They rowed long into the night. Lanterns were lit to provide a dismal light for the prisoners. Skarde's stomach grumbled long and mighty before several of the crew's bullies came to feed the rowers.

Skarde was handed a bowl of coarse grey gruel and took a long swig from an unclean water bladder. He ate – a dissatisfied scowl on his face, but he ate. Marus struggled to get his food down, and at length his bowl was snatched from his hands before he could finish.

"Let him eat," Skarde said.

"He's had his due," the bully said in an eastern accent of Sharoshan, trade language of the Southern Seas. "Feed him like a mother bird next time if you worry over him."

"Your name is Erbiz, is it not?" Skarde sneered, having heard some of the crew's banter.

"Aye," Erbiz said. "To my crewmates, it is. To you, it is Master. And you, to me, are but a chained slave. Your tone carries a threat. A fool's threat. Now, sleep, both of you, or face the lash."

Skarde's face flushed hot with anger. His hand moved reflexively to grasp his sword hilt – but of course it had been taken along with all his other possessions. Though Erbiz could no doubt not see his redness in the dim light, he could read it in Skarde's flashing eyes. The bully laughed like a hyena and left him to stew.

"It's no use," Marus said. He crawled to the floor and shifted about trying to find relief.

Skarde pursed his lips and listened to the waves lapping at the hull. That sound conjured thoughts of roaming, unbound and wild, with traders and reavers both. It meant freedom. He took the chain in his hands and pulled 'til his muscles swelled to bursting. The chains held, as he knew they would, but he wouldn't be able to sleep without an attempt.

He lay flat on the wooden deck. The ship was well built, and the boards were smooth. He had slept in much worse conditions, and he found rest easy enough. Marus, however, groaned and shifted through the night. His injuries brought pain, and the shifting sea did nothing to help his comfort. As men labor, their anguish is overlooked, but when resting discomfort is magnified to agony. Skarde slept with one eye cracked half open as he always did. He sensed that Marus tossed and turned throughout the night, tormented and restless.

Skarde awoke as three of the bullies began kicking and whipping slaves to awaken them. He shot them grim looks as he seated himself on the bench and awaited rowing orders. He shook and swore at Marus to arise, lest he suffer a further injury. Marus clambered up the bench and gripped the oar, more to steady himself than to row. His eyes swam.

The drum beat out its monotonous pace again and the ship tore through the water. *To where?* Skarde wondered. He swore as Marus slowly slumped, his rowing weaker and weaker. Skarde took his slack, but it was not enough. As he feared, a bully took notice. Skarde glanced up to see Erbiz looming over Marus.

"Put your back into it, worm!" Erbiz spat, striking Marus cruelly across his back.

Marus let out a strangled cry. Erbiz struck him again, and Marus shook with effort trying to pull the oar.

"Let go of the oar, you big savage," Erbiz said to Skarde, brandishing his lash. "Let him row for a while."

Skarde brows wrinkled in disgust. "None of the 'savages' of my village treated an injured man so. Let's see your bravado when chains do not restrain those you beat!"

Erbiz laughed and struck hard. Marus gasped in agony as blood trickled down his back. "I've killed men your size, you ape. 'Tis not my job, now, to teach you a lesson in civility. My job is to see that you row."

Marus pulled at the oar but could not keep pace without Skarde's assistance. Erbiz watched and shook his head, his eyes gloated morbidly. Marus kept up a valiant effort but shook with pain. Skarde thought Erbiz might beat Marus or himself, but he simply walked away. Skarde grabbed the oar and rowed. The eyes of every slave on the deck turned silently toward them, apprehension written in their tightly pulled features. There was some discussion above deck among the officers, though Skarde could not make out any details.

Presently, several crewmen descended the stairs followed by a man Skarde took to be the captain. Skarde saw his boots first as he descended the steep stairs from the upper deck. Rugged and practical but kept spotless. He stood chest out when he reached the rowing deck, and surveyed the slaves – all glancing his way, many with a hint of fear. He wore a red tabard over fine leather armour, a red cape, and a cap like those worn by naval officers of southern fleets. His high cheekbones and piercing blue eyes were rare among the olive-skinned men of the south.

The captain strode the deck, his back straight and his head held high, examining each man with a flicker of his eyes. Skarde nudged Marus to straighten, and with a shaking effort, he did so. The captain passed Skarde and Marus, strolling to the back of the deck and completing his inspection. He turned like he was grinding something underneath his boot. He marched back, his boots the footsteps of doom in Skarde's ear. He halted beside them and loomed over Marus. Skarde's compatriot trembled as he stiffened his back. Skarde kept his gaze forward. He grit his teeth and dared not challenge the captain with his eyes or with sharp words, for Marus' sake. On the salt air, he smelled death. The captain made a quick gesture. Skarde disliked the hyena smile that spread over Erbiz' face.

"Aye, Captain Basan," Erbiz said.

He and another took hold of Marus and unlocked his manacles. They dragged the staggering man down the deck and up the stairs. Skarde's blood heated. He looked the captain in the eyes with knotted brows, and the captain held his gaze with a curious look. Skarde did not have to wonder long what fate Marus faced. Above decks, there was a scuffle, a scream, and a splash.

Skarde leapt to his feet and heaved at the rattling chains. "You black-heart! You dog!" Skarde shouted, spittle on his lips. "What fiend slays a man who needed only a few days rest?"

The remaining bully raised his whip to strike Skarde, but the captain interposed his hand.

"Nay, striking this fool will avail us nothing," Captain Basan said to his man. "I was once like you. Like all of you," He caught Skarde's eyes again before gesturing wide to all the chained rowers. "A vagabond. A sellsword. Finding coin wherever I might."

He walked back down the aisle, catching the eyes of any who dared to look at him. All turned their gaze away from his, save for Skarde. "And those of you who toiled for your coin in walled cities, do not imagine you had a greater purpose than his. You all worked for snakes! For cowards, greedy men, and fat indolent merchants. Why? For a better time to come? Pah! Only for more filth to come; more cowardly, more greedy, more indolent!"

His eyes blazed like a fanatic's, and his hands flew through the air, emphasizing every point. Skarde held his tongue. He knew not how he might naysay such fervor without steel.

"Now, I fight for the glory of the Iron Brotherhood! Here is no place for the sluggard. And though you all shall toil, in field or in rock, your purpose is higher than the petty kings of the Earth. For the Master of the Iron Brotherhood seeks a higher destiny and shall order the whole world to that Great Purpose! Do not lament the chains upon your body. They are less heavy than the chains about your soul, from which you are already freed."

He stood tall and swept his gaze over his audience as if looking for challenge. Finding none, he trod away with pomp and scaled the stair. The slaves remained frozen in place until the bully cracked the whip and demanded they row.

I must take my leave at the earliest chance! Skarde resolved.

Days of relentless rowing wore the captives down, in both body and resolve. Skarde, used to sea travel and long campaigning, fared as well as any of them, but he too yearned for a change of scene. Presently, something caught his eye. He ceased rowing and bent over to glance out of the oarlock hole in the hull of the trireme. Something had fluttered by. *A seabird? Hodan, may Funir bring me a sign that land is near!* He rested his hands just for a moment, feeling his fingers throb. Taking a moment to listen, he heard only the ocean waters lapping against the wooden hull. His musing was cut short by the sudden snap of a lash. Pain lanced across the bare skin of his back.

"Keep rowing, slave!" barked Erbiz.

Skarde gritted his teeth, refusing to cry out or even wince at the blow. He gripped the oar once again with his calloused hands and his mighty sinews strained. He threshed the sea in silence 'til the looming slaver swaggered further down the deck. *Damn his whip hand!*

"Did ye see anything, Skarde?" said the captive seated behind him.

"Aye, I'm certain," he said. "Just the flash of a wing."

"Once my feet are planted on solid land, I'll give them ten blows for every one they gave me," the man said.

Skarde's lips pressed together in a grim smile. How many others were ready for a fight? How many other fools, beside himself, were seized in the dockside drinking pits of Byzerdamen? They could make real trouble, if given half a chance. Skarde let the mad thought stew in his mind. *Unarmed, what chance might we have against sword wielding sea-dogs?* Still, his pulse quickened.

An hour passed and he oft stooped to catch a glimpse outside the crescent left between the hole and the oar. Something fluttered in the sky. Soon after shouts from above signaled something of interest. Skarde strained to hear. He held his breath and ceased to row. Through the creaking oars, the hiss of the wind, and the sound of the sea Skarde was sure he heard that jackal of a captain bellow orders.

"Be quick... already late..." was all his ears could catch before Erbiz snapped his whip again at him. Skarde sneered at the pain and muttered a threat of retribution. The bully kept on shouting instructions and hardly heard him. The air was filled with excitement, and his fellow captives looked about anxiously.

A grinding hiss emanated from the hull itself, and several of Skarde's fellows nearly jumped. Erbiz laughed at their distress and braced himself against a mast pole as the hiss returned and the trireme lurched to a halt.

"They've beached the ship!" Skarde said.

Presently, four of the crew descended from the top deck, swords drawn, and two more began freeing slaves from their chains. At first, they were unfettered and disembarked two by two, starting at the bow and moving back. There were calls for swiftness, and so six, then twelve were taken at once. Then, they loosed as many as they could, prodding them forward with their weapons.

"Luwydi!" Skarde could hardly believe his luck as he shuffled along.

He glanced at the other slaves he deemed fighting men and caught a gleam in their eyes. He topped the deck, and bright sunlight all but blinded him. A gangplank was heavy with trudging slaves before him, and as he set foot on it, he noticed a sea-dog on the sand right below him. With a sword, he waved the line onward toward flustered crew-men tying the wrists of slaves with rope as fast as they could.

There was no chance to prepare a plan. He simply jumped at the opportunity... and straight off the gangplank.

Skarde dropped square onto the swordsman. He crumpled to the ground under Skarde's massive weight, and Skarde dove for the sword. The man was no lightweight, and though dazed, he gripped his weapon with the tenacity of a soldier. Even as Skarde struggled for the weapon, the other enslaved fighting men leapt down to the beach to grapple a foeman.

Skarde punched his opponent, but another warrior charged him. He sprang back, scooped up a handful of sand, and threw it into his attacker's face. The swordsman staggered back, but Skarde knew that he had only bought himself a few seconds. The situation was hopeless.

He ran and hoped others would follow his lead.

Dashing across the beach toward a jungle, he risked a quick look behind. The melee spread across the beach. Several slaves were sprinting in one direction or another. The swordsman, in whose face he had cast sand, was making straight for him. He sprinted across the shifting sand, and even as the thick canopy of jungle loomed near the thrill of escape was tempered by the desperation of his flight. *Might I escape? If this be their territory...* his hand felt suddenly empty for want of a sword. A desperate ploy sprang into his head and as the shadows covered him, he dove into a thick bush just off the trail and hid.

Drubbing footsteps came near, and Skarde held his breath in his bellows-like chest. *A fool's plan!* Skarde chastised himself.

The enemy soldier loomed close. If caught, Skarde would die... and then his foe barrelled passed him. Skarde's powerful legs launched him forward, and he sprang at the swordsman like a great hunting cat. His foe swung his sword back in an arc, but a moment to late. Skarde caught the man's wrist, and a struggle for the sword began in earnest. Though larger, Skarde failed to rip the weapon out of the man's grasp. Here was no untested soldier – the hardened muscles and scars on his body spoke much.

Desperate, Skarde held the sword at bay, and then slammed his right fist into his opponent's face in a brutal burst. He roared like an enraged beast and smote his foe 'til blood poured down his face. The soldier stumbled back and Skarde ripped the sword from his grip. He slammed the pommel into the man's temple like a bolt, and the dog collapsed to the ground.

Chapter Two

Skarde looked at the solid blade in his hands and tossed his head back in a roar of laughter. "You thought me a big fool, aye?" Skarde said to unhearing ears.

The man carried no obvious supplies. Still, Skarde bent down to look for a coin purse. As a lone traveler in strange lands, he would not turn away such opportunities. Yet, he grumbled and stood still. *Where might I find taverns, wenches, and wine here? And coins might jingle.*

"Keep your pennies, friend," he said to the corpse. "You might need them in Hell."

Skarde peered back to the shore through the thick jungle leaves. The trireme was still surrounded by the chaos Skarde had caused. Men – slaver and slave – still fought and gave chase. *How unwise it was for them to unshackle so many of us from the oars before they restrained us further,* Skarde thought. *And how foolish that I hid in wait to attack an armed foe. Yet here I am.*

He turned and ran as fast as he did before his weapon was won. The fight had not been a quiet affair, and he doubted not some swift footed warrior – if not many of them – would soon be on his trail. So, he ran, heedless and swift into the jungle, uncaring of the trail of broken foliage he left. He ran 'til he was breathless, and a little further still.

At last, he halted. Sparing a moment to catch his breath, he took stock of his whereabouts. He only now noticed that while running through the jungle maze he had climbed some height over a twisted path. His line-of-sight blocked by a few troublesome fronds, he could see now over the green canopy to the sea. With his sharp eyes, far off down the shore, he could just make out the masts of the slave ship. Below him was a path. At least a path as could be called in these parts. It was not more than a track cleared of the most impassable foliage. Skarde stood utterly silent and listened. The jungle spoke. Strange birds sang and some unknown beast hooted and whistled. There was no trace of human voice or footstep. They were out there, he knew, despite the silence.

He had planned no further ahead than to run, to flee into the dense jungle to try his luck there. *What now?* He considered another ambush right where he was. *It is too good a spot*, he thought. *They will know it. They will come up behind me. Yet if they are many, they might be confident and take the quickest path, or be careless...*

He searched for stones to throw. There was little to find in the forest duff but at last he found two fist-sized rocks. *I shall hole up for a few more minutes*, he thought. *If they give me a shot, I mean to take it.*

The tense moments were like hours. Every rustle in the vegetation sent a tingle up his spine. After too long a time to wait safely, his sharp ears caught movement behind him. He turned with sly restraint born of experience. He saw nothing, but heard a rustle deep in the bushes. His senses tingling, he caught sight of a dog-sized primate moving among the trees. The monkey stared curiously at him. Skarde left it to its own so as not to attract attention. It might even hoot and holler should someone flank him.

Too late it was for any other consideration. As he turned his eyes back to the path, his pursuers were upon him. Skarde guessed that they must have been moving fast to be upon him so soon, but now stalked forward with caution. *They know the jungle*, he thought. There were six of them. Three with blades drawn in front and behind were three with bows at the ready. Skarde's eyebrows furrowed, and his blood ran hot as their faces became evident. Captain Basan, without his brightly colored cloak, took the lead, and behind him was the petty tyrant Erbiz. Their eyes glanced up, but they did not see him. He was as still as a tiger about to pounce.

There was no time to consider the tactical advantage of aiming for a swordsman or a bowman. He stood and hurled a stone with a ferocity and skill practiced since his childhood in a land of grim mountains. Bowmen were, by his belief, cowardly but deadly. He aimed at the head of the middle bowman. It struck true, with a wet crunch and a flash of blood. He fell to the ground like a sack of wet flour.

The bowman behind Skarde's target screamed a warning. In a flash, the leading bowman spun and shot at him. Skarde had hoped he would have a moment to throw his second stone. In mid throw he was forced to drop low, and the bowman's arrow cut the foliage in which he hid, far too close for his comfort. He popped up from his crouch right away to make his throw. The bowman had already knocked another arrow. Skarde hurled the stone without a moment to aim. His shot was almost off, but it struck the bowman in the shoulder. The bowman yelled a curse and mis-shot an arrow far above him. The three swordsmen were halfway up the steep slope that civilized men could scarce hope to cling. The middle bowman abandoned the care of his fellow to stand and take aim. Skarde turned and ran even as another arrow sliced by.

"Haha," he laughed in mockery. "Two for me, none for you!"

He bolted into the bushes behind him. At once, his watchful monkey companion retreated before him, howling to its fellows. The jungle erupted in heckling calls. Hundreds of primates screamed at the intrusion upon their territory and began throwing heavy hard-shelled fruits, sticks, and feces down at him.

"I thought we had an understanding!" He yelled back.

Sprinting, his long legs carried him quicker than the shorter brutes behind him. He kept at the forefront of the aerial assault, and as he dashed out of the tree devil's feeding ground, he chanced slowing for a look behind. Four of his captors were chasing after him – or rather were trying. They fought off a wave of simian attackers. Outnumbered ten to one, they swung their swords desperately to ward off an armory's worth of sticks and branches. The foul tempered monkeys charged them, flailed at them with their primitive weapons, and retreated as yet more took their swings.

Skarde laughed uproariously and kept running.

He felt a thrill of delight at his luck. *Still*, he thought, *I doubt a pack of monkeys will dispatch my foes for me. May they be bruised and befouled before they continue to harass me, by Thunir!* As the jungle became even less passable, he wondered about the last four foes, or five if the second bowman was able to continue. He felt a fluster as the trail all but disappeared.

"By the Nine Hells," he cursed. "Let's have done with this chase!"

Skarde spun and dove off the path. Running through the thick jungle undergrowth for some hundred paces, he turned back the way he had come, off the path he had left. *I've had more than my share of luck,* he thought. *I must make more than the most of it.* He pumped his legs as fast as he could with no care for stealth. His enemy would likely now be done with the primates, though he could still hear a fearsome ruckus in the distance. He blundered out of the jungle into the primates' glade, and nigh gave away his position. On sudden, he dropped low to the ground and scanned the area through the leaves. His four pursuers were retreating from the small army of monkeys, backing their way onto the forest path on which he had escaped minutes ago. Were their backs not turned, he surely would have been spotted.

Skarde watched silent and unmoving. They fought off a ferocious attack, and several of the monkeys were cut apart. This sent the rest into a hooting frenzy, but they stayed their assault. The four backed defensively away into the jungle. Skarde laughed silently at his foes, but didn't defy the primates by treading again on their territory. He wasted no time in pressing toward his original path through the almost impassable tangle. He was pulled and scratched in every conceivable place as he made his way. He hoped to come up behind the four. The noise from the tribe of monkeys was now ear-splitting. It masked his movement... but also theirs.

As he closed in on what he reckoned must be their path, he slowed and stopped. Skarde strained to listen and heard the shouts of men between the hoots. He could not make out what they were saying, though he thought it likely they were arguing about where he was, and the merits of caution or speed.

His fingers rubbed restlessly against his new-won sword's hilt. Now would be as good a time as any to attack. He struggled forward as fast as the devilish snarls under foot would allow. He burst out on to the path and the almost-gone trail he left seemed as broad as a king's highway. Quickly catching his bearings, he ran along. He hoped that his foe still conversed, and that the diminished cacophony of monkeys would still cover his footfalls. He planned to run for two or three minutes, then slow to a more cautious pace. But Luwydi, the God of Mischief, withdrew his favor. A moment before Skarde planned to stop and listen, he rounded a foliage draped turn and found himself upon them.

The bowman was at their rear. He spotted Skarde first. There was a momentary flash of surprise in his eyes as the huge blonde warrior seemed to have burst out of the bush behind him. He spun. In a whirlwind of action, he knocked and drew an arrow. Skarde was upon him, roaring like a beast. His arrow flew as Skarde's forearm battered the bow aside. The arrow flew, not at Skarde's heart as the bowman intended, but it drew blood still – the arrowhead slashed along Skarde's shoulder. Skarde's thick muscled arm brought the sword down upon his foe and cleaved his head clean from his body. A fountain of hot blood shot skyward as his head dropped to the ground like a slab of wet meat. The three swordsmen spun in disbelief. A moment of horrific silence withheld screams of rage that suddenly pierced the air.

They sprang at Skarde, though he had already turned to race back along the meager path. He dared a quick glance over his shoulder, being careful not to break his stride. His long legs carried him swiftly. After a few dozen strides, he glanced again. He was outpacing them save for one who ran a tremendous race.

To fight or run? Thought Skarde.

Ahead was a large tree with a huge, exposed root which held back a tall ledge of earth five feet from the path. He glanced back again and guessed how fast he might run so they would meet at that tree. Gritting his teeth, he slowed. Near the tree, he burst off the trail, put his boot on the ledge, and kicked off from it with all the might of his thews.

"Yahhh!" He roared as he turned on his pursuer.

The swift warrior was closer than Skarde expected, but was all the more taken off guard. He had hardly raised his sword for a down stroke when Skarde was upon him. Skarde grabbed the warrior's sword arm in a flash to hold back his downward stroke, and he stabbed at his guts. He struck a grievous cut as the two collided. Skarde lost his grip on his sword as he fell away from his foe. Thrown back on his rump, he watched as the swordsman staggered back, clutching at his spilled guts in a tide of red.

Skarde looked up, the thrill of his victory short lived. Captain Basan and Erbiz were not far behind and would be upon him in a mere moment. His sword out of reach, he spun about to make a desperate dash into the jungle without a weapon when his eyes widened.

"Funir's Wing!" He laughed fiercely.

The impact had hurled the dying swordsman's weapon behind Skarde. It lay on the ground but a few feet away. He scrambled for it and picked it up and dashed away. As quickly as he had flew away, he stopped and turned on his pursuers. He lashed out with his newly acquired sword and roared. The two warriors nearly tripped over each other as they halted. Skarde lashed out at Basan to take advantage of their momentary clumsiness. His blow was parried away as the swords clanged. The swordsman reversed his stroke, stabbing at Skarde's face. He jerked his head back and the blade missed him by inches. Had the strike been aimed lower, he would have been gutted. Skarde skated to the side and tried to regain his footing, but Erbiz swept down with a diagonal stroke. Almost toppled, Skarde rolled over his shoulder and sprang up as Basan came at him with cautious, testing strikes. Erbiz began maneuvering around his side.

"You won't catch me that easy, dogs!" Skarde said with a snarl.

With eyes like blue fire, he circled around Basan, and away from Erbiz. He strove to keep one behind the other, lest he fight two at once or be struck down from behind. They circled one another for what seemed like long minutes. They traded tentative blows 'til Erbiz, tiring of the game, rushed him.

He stabbed out, but Skarde swept it aside. Captain Basan sprang forward to chop down viciously. Skarde had no time to reverse his sword. He sprang at his attacker and brought his elbow up, connecting with his foe's jaw. He would have brought a sword stroke down on him, but Erbiz swept out wildly and Skarde just managed to block the attack. With a frustrated growl, he vaulted back, wary of a blow from behind.

The Captain, however, was staggered. Skarde moved towards him hoping for an opportunity to strike him before he recovered, but Erbiz rained down wild strokes. It was a distraction, Skarde knew, to protect his fellow. If he struck, he would be defenseless for a deadly moment. Skarde moved back on to the path and kept away from both.

"We kill you slowly," said Erbiz. "You'll not leave this island with your limbs."

"I'll kill you all," Skarde roared.

"There are a thousand of us," the swordsman laughed.

"Once I cut off your ugly heads," he said, "you'll be a thousand less six."

"You will not trick us again," Erbiz spat.

"I've no need!"

Skarde swung his sword in a fury. His foe gave ground, parrying as best he could, his eyes wide at the mad blows. Basan was blinking and trying to focus on him. At least one on one, it was a fair fight. Despite his boasting, Skarde well knew that facing two hardened fighters in terrain they were familiar with was a poor bet. With a roar, he battered his opponent with thunderous blows. His foe scrambled back as Skarde pressed his advantage of size and strength. Erbiz defended himself expertly, and other than a flash of fear in his eyes, he was unharmed. He managed to retreat back to his fellow. The captain had recovered and swung at him. Skarde was forced to retreat.

"Nine Hells!" Skarde yelled.

He fought off stings from left and right and was pushed back into the dense foliage. *I will fall unless I...*

He stumbled back and dropped to the ground. Captain Basan reared up for a downward stroke at his exposed neck. But Skarde's legs were well grounded. He had feinted, not fallen. Skarde leapt at his foe and his sword arced upward, cutting his foe from crotch to neck. Blood poured from a long gash like a hellish waterfall. The wounded captain rigidly stumbled back, his eyes stark open, his sword still held high as he toppled across the path.

Erbiz let out a blood curdling shriek and flew at him, bashing his sword against Skarde's blade with all the ferocity Skarde had shown him. Skarde kept back. He parried and stepped smoothly out of range. He let the frenzied warrior swing himself to exhaustion. As his strokes became more desperate, Skarde halted his retreat and gave a few counter strokes. At last, the furious warrior charged him and swung a close blow. Skarde parried and reversed his swing. It sliced along his belly. The swordsman hopped back and clutched at himself, yet he stood. Blood there was, but Skarde knew the stroke was not fatal by the lack of resistance he had felt. Erbiz laughed and pointed his sword at the exasperated Northman.

"Now die!" Erbiz said.

He bounded at Skarde, his blade spinning. He brought another stroke down but the Skarde slipped away. They traded blows and Skarde leapt forward, quick as a tiger, with a battle cry. The warrior stumbled back and raised his sword with both hands to receive a thunderous blow. Skarde chanced a deep strike even though it left his foe an opening. His blade whistled through the thick air and struck a heavy blow. The warrior's sword spun off and fell to the earth, along with his hands, still gripping the hilt.

Erbiz held up his bloody stumps and let out a quavering scream of horror. He stared at Skarde like a mad thing before turning and running back along the path toward the primate's glade.

Skarde fought the urge to give chase and strike him down. He was no longer a threat, and he doubted not that there were other foes somewhere in the jungle.

He yelled in triumph, holding his sword aloft. "Run back to your master with your tail between your legs, dog, and tell him he is next!"

Chapter Three

Satisfied with his insult, Skarde looted the three nearby bodies. Among them, they carried few items of use. He recovered two knives – poor for fighting but well-made and utilitarian. He stripped one body of a belt to carry a sword, daggers, and their scabbards. He found a half empty gourd of weak ale. That, he drained on the spot. Fighting was damnable thirsty work. He picked up the least blood-spattered sword. He swung it in his hands and tested its feel against the one he held.

"These are fine blades," he whispered to himself.

He scrutinized them and noted that they were some of the best workmanship he had ever seen. They, and the two swords on the ground, were practically identical and no doubt made by the same smith. *Where would these pirates acquire such masterworks?* He kept both the swords, holding one in each hand as he continued down the path. A cold trail he desired to leave for those hunting him. With a little less haste and a careful eye, he walked. He needed the lay of the land. Soon, he would need food and shelter.

As Skarde delved further into this green hell, his shoulder pained him hotly. He saw he had been bleeding, but now rivulets of sweat stung the eight-inch gash. Upon closer inspection, he saw it was shallow, but unclean and ripe for infection. Grumbling, he walked on and kept an eye out for large leaves. There was little at ground level, though far above him there was a bounty. At last, the canopy faltered, and he found suitable leaves within reach. He stopped to collect a few, and dabbed the dirt, blood, and sweat away as best he could. *I hope these will not inflame my wound further,* he thought.

The green canopy reasserted itself and then broke again. Far off he saw, in the opening sky, a vapor rising. He climbed steadily, and ahead there was some peak still shrouded in foliage. He kept moving, and his thoughts turned to water. He could manage a few miserable days without food, but the jungle was hot, oppressive, and sweaty – thirst would take its toll. He came across a trickling creek. It had a dun and milky hue. Disliking it, he turned his thirsty thoughts away from it. He left the meager trail to follow its course.

The rivulet led to another which joined to another and another. In just a thousand paces, it joined a considerable stream and soon that tumbled down a twenty-foot waterfall. Without a fire to boil water, he would have to chance illness drinking directly from a stream. He had no pot, and the wet raw wood he might be able to gather, if he could even manage to get it to burn, would send up smoke visible for miles. The waterfall seemed as wholesome a source as he might find. At the very least he could wash away the blood, dirt, and weeks worth of salt and sweat.

He skirted the rise from which the waterfall toppled and climbed down. At the edge of the pool that lay beneath it, he stripped and made his way through the knee-deep water toward the fall. In his right hand, he still held a sword. Here, he would not let a moment pass without a weapon.

The blasting cool water renewed him right away. The oppressive air of the jungle that seemed to cling to his skin was now dispelled. He swung his sword into the onrushing waters. He felt he could fight the rest of the thousand warriors. The cold water bit the cut in his shoulder, but he bore it gladly. He rinsed blood and filth from his breeches and filled the gourd with water. He eyed the filled water sack with mistrust. Only would he drink if thirst overcame him. Until then, he might find fruits or some other refreshment. He left the pool, squeezed the water from his clothes, and got dressed. *Must not tarry*, he thought. They would sooner or later check all nearby watering holes. He aimed to put miles behind him.

He followed one meager path after another. He would have preferred travel through an unmarked way, but the jungle was too slow a trudge. He rose on the western side of a low mountain. From some unseen crevasse near its cone-like peak, vapors rose. He looked and wondered. There were geysers and volcanoes in his homeland far to the north which were said to throw steams, vapors, ash, and fire into the air. He had not seen them though. Lost in wonder, he took too-long a moment looking on in reverie. *Perhaps another time*, he thought.

He climbed higher and northward on the mountain 'til the sun began to descend. He had found a few berry bushes of a kind he had seen in the south and ate of them.

"These quench neither hunger nor thirst," he grumbled, "but they are better than grumbles alone."

The trail began to even off, even dip occasionally, and the lands to the north unfolded. He set off northward even as the sun touched the horizon. Here, closer to the peak, the jungle was thinner, and the ground drier. *Better*, he thought, *than places below for a place to lie for the night.* He found a sandy nook in the embrace of a root of a tall tree. There he lay, sword in hand, as darkness settled on the land. His eyes scanned the deepening shadows, and he braced himself for an unpleasant night.

Skarde had long been accustomed to sleeping with one eye open. He rested in fitful stretches; the hoots and screeches of night creatures were of little concern. He awoke once at the slithering of a thick rope like form down the same root he slept under. A snake, barely visible against the stars above, had come to investigate. Despite its significant size, Skarde was too large a dinner. He did not expect it to attack him, but still his hand gripped the handle of a knife. At long last, dawn broke. Skarde was up before the sun. His mouth was dry, and his eyes stung.

He groaned a yawn loudly. Above him a small monkey eyed him warily.

"No worse than a night of drinking," he said to it. "Farewell."

He picked up the gourd and weighed his need. *Not yet.* He hung it from his belt and continued down the trail. The sun rose in the sky and sweat dappled his skin. Past noon, he chanced upon another stream and followed its course 'til the jungle thickened again. Just as the floor on either side of the path became impassable, he saw a group of trees to his right that bore heavy fruit almost the size of his head. They were flattened ovals and bright orange. He had seen large fruits like these before, though smaller and paler. Those had a fibrous meat and sweet water inside hard shells. He ran his leathery tongue over his dry lips and trudged through the clinging underbrush to the copse of trees.

Gripping the rough trunk, he judged his chances. He was a born climber, but his was a land of hills and mountains, not tropical trees. Still, he grappled the trunk and kicked off. Not without effort, he climbed the tree. The swords made the climb awkward, but he managed. As he settled near the fruits, he saw a handful of gigantic fist sized spiders. Pulling out a knife, he pushed them out of the way with the flat of the blade. He found with a tap that the fruits were hard shelled. He cut a group of four away, slicing through a tough rope like stalk. The fruits clattered to the ground.

He descended and hacked his way through a tough hide with his knife. He ate. The meat of the fruit was heavy, fibrous, and dry. Its taste was milky sweet, but there was far too little moisture. He sucked at it, and after a labor, he had hardly wetted his mouth.

He spat the dry wad from his mouth. "A curse on this foul jungle!"

He marched off, hoping to find some more useful fruit or another source of water. After hours of travel, and slick with sweat, he found little but a few berries again. He stopped for a while under the shadow of a tree and waited out the heat of the day. *If one of my hunters catches up with me*, he thought, *I hope he has the hospitality to die with a full ale skin on him.*

The sun slid across the half-hidden sky, and Skarde's legs were restless. At last, he stood and continued. His muscles began to ache. He had hoped to last a little longer, but the heat was draining him. The land became rockier as the evening wore on. It was then he saw wisps of smoke in the distance. He passed some rocky outcroppings that he thought might hide caves. *Perhaps a fair place to settle for the night*, he thought. However, he wanted a closer look at the sources of the smoke first. He traveled another mile down the path, and the ground became rockier 'til it led to a ledge. He was a good hundred feet over the jungle below. Amid the trees were groupings of unassuming huts and long fields of tended crops. A few farmers and work animals in the fields were completing the last tasks of the day.

Skarde dropped low to the ground. He knew not whose eyes might be looking up at him. With his sharp eyes, he made out a dozen slender but sturdy folk carrying baskets, leading animals, or stacking away tools. He saw no sign of weapons. *Who are these people*, he wondered? *Do they serve the pirates? Might I bargain for... or otherwise obtain, water and food?*

He thought it best not to enter their village at dusk. He went back along the path to the caves to spend what he hoped was a less wretched night. *Perhaps rested thoughts will light a path of action.*

He arrived at the cave and sat against the wall. His legs groaned as he bent them.

"Ahh!" he called out, his voice a wheezy croak.

Dizziness addled him as he settled back. The stifling jungle took a cruel toll even on his tireless constitution. He held up his gourd and sighed. *I must chance it.*

He uncorked it and turned it to his cracked lips. Never did a swampy swill taste so sweet. The water flowed down his throat like nectar. Draining it, he fell into a dull sleep. He tossed with troubled dreams and awoke suddenly gripped by sickness. He fought against his heaving stomach as he stumbled out of his low hanging shelter. There, he threw up, and worse. He retched again and again 'til he wondered if even his guts were left in him. *I've been worse off after a night of drink*, he thought. *Just need water...* He collapsed on the bare rock.

He awoke, baking in the hot morning sun. *Move or die.*

He stumbled to his feet and moved like one half dead toward the village. The night had brought no clear thoughts as he had hoped, but it had brought clear purpose. He might find what he needed in the village, or he might not, but the jungle offered only death by thirst and sickness. *And if I am attacked in the village I will at least die with a sword in hand*, he thought.

He kept shambling on 'til he passed the outcrop from which he looked upon the village. Even now, in the early morning light, he saw the fields busy with farmers. He kept on 'til he came across another waterfall. Beside it was a steep slope of jutting rocks. Here, he chose to climb down. A foot-path around could be miles off. Already his mind was reeling. He slipped and lost his grip, and only just caught himself. He cursed dryly. It was a climb that otherwise would have been little challenge. He staggered to balance as he dropped the final few feet and stood for a moment in the cool spray of the falls.

Trudging toward the village he found a well-trod path. He threw caution to the wind and took that route unhidden. Every fifty paces or so, he came across foot-tall, brightly painted clay figurines. He smiled with cracked lips. *Spirits to guard the path?* he thought. *Will they guard mine?* It was then he noticed his two swords' scabbards knocking at his thighs. *A burden, but more sure a guard than any spirit.*

Was the village further off than he had seen, or were his legs slow? At long last, he caught sight of an open field far off through an opening in the trees. Bolstered, he picked up his pace. Then, tipping a small rise, he caught sight of a young boy of about twelve walking toward him a hundred paces ahead. He bore a thin yoke on his shoulders, and from that hung four gourds that swung lightly as if unfilled. The boy froze and gave him a wary look.

"Boy! Boy, wait!" he called out, though his voice was more like sand rubbed on wood than human.

He ran as best he could, hoping to speak with him. "Boy, wait!" he croaked again.

The boy tossed his yoke aside and ran like a deer back the way he had come. Skarde followed. His long legs would have easily overtaken the lad, but they failed. He fell to the ground and the world seemed to tumble about him. There, with the cruel sun beating down on him, he lay unmoving.

He recalled little save for a vague feeling of a struggle against hot bonds in the dark. They seemed to tear at his flesh and strangle him. He opened his eyes. He was dizzy and lying on a patch of rough straw. Voices. He felt trapped between the world of waking and of sleep, but he began to focus on two voices. One was stern but calm, the other frantic. He was in a small hut. It had one small door open to the overly bright sky outside. The voices were arguing. Skarde did not speak the language but often the frantic voice repeated a phrase – "Sahiyno avan-de! Sahiyno avan-de!" – with a tremble of fear.

The voices of the men stopped suddenly, and the doorway was filled with a dark silhouette against the burning sky. His hand by habit reached for the pommel of his sword... where was it?

"Najata," The shadowed figure said. The voice of an elder yet strong and deep. "You speak Sharoshan?

"Yes," Skarde said.

He walked into the hut and knelt beside Skarde. He was an elderly man with long white hair. His muscles were as strappy as the boy who had fled from him earlier, but his skin was a weather beaten brown and as wrinkled as an alligator.

"I Pyae. You drink bad water. Bad water make sick. Maybe die. You drink medicine. Maybe no die."

The old man held up a thin leather drinking bladder. "Drink."

Skarde struggled halfway up and took the skin in his shaking hands. He drank lustily. The liquid had a kick to it and was a delicate milky sweet taste. He drank it to its last drop and his body burned as if he had downed whiskey.

"Ahh!" he croaked, "It is good."

"You rest now," Pyae said.

Skarde struggled to remain resting on his elbow. He saw that his swords were strewn on the ground. He had a vague memory of dropping them there. No one had even touched them. Through his swimming senses, he saw he was in a supply hut by the edge of a field. There were stools, small packets of food, and water skins among a few other small personal items. His straw mat was at the edge opposite the door. His swords would be in the way for those moving about the small space, yet there they lay. *Do the villagers fear to touch them?* He thought.

"Why do you help me?"

Pyae shrugged. "Some listen to star watcher. See one big star fall from sky, then many small star. Star watcher say stranger come make big change. Small star fall like Sahiyno fall."

"Sahiyno," Skarde echoed. The situation became clearer in his muddled mind. They were the slavers.

"Ah," Pyae said. His eyes looked about as one searching for words. He gestured at Skarde's weapons on the ground.

"Sword," Skarde said.

Pyae nodded. "Sword-man. Some think you come – get rid of all sword-man."

"You believe that?" Skarde said.

"Yes. No," Pyae shrugged. "Bad... 'Niyah'... to let man die of thirst."

"My thanks," Skarde said. "Do the swordsmen threaten you?"

"Sword-man come. Bad men. Take food. Here." Pyae said, gesturing to the land about him. "There... There..." He said gesturing to the distance. Skarde took that gesture to mean other villages.

Skarde held the man's gaze as best he could. "I am a danger to you and your people. If the swordsmen come and find me..." He struggled to get up.

The old man laughed. "You here or no, sword-man still danger."

He planted a hand on Skarde's chest and pushed him back down. "Medicine make you sleep. You leave, you fall in field. You too big to carry again."

"Thank you, Pyae. I am fit to...." He rolled to his knees and struggled to stand. "... and strong..." He bent to pick up his swords, toppled, and did not rise again that day.

Chapter Four

Skarde clawed his way through a nightmare of pain and choking. Light pierced his eyelids, and the dull redness chased the phantoms away. He lay still, breathing quick and shallow, covered in sweat. Shouts in the distance touched his ears over his breathing, then a crack of a whip. His eyes flew open. He sat up and struggled as the dimly lit hut spun. Dropping to his hands and knees, he crawled to the open door. Pulling himself up on the door frame, he hid behind the wall. He peered out and winced at the morning light.

From his vantage, he could see across the field twenty or so soldiers in black cloaks harassing villagers. Pyae pleaded with one of the soldiers. A young lad, not yet of twenty summers, drudged toward a wagon the soldiers had left on the road with a heavy wrapped package strapped to his back. A soldier barked orders and the young man slowed and gave the soldier a defiant look. Right away, the soldier was on him, beating him with a long thin switch. The young man tried to dodge it and gave the soldier a kick, but the favor was returned with a mailed fist. The young man fell, and two more soldiers came over, only to laugh.

Skarde's jaw clenched. He could not stop them. Even if he slew them, he did not doubt that a gang of the ruffians would descend on the village and wreak bloody revenge. Pyae hurried forward and begged the soldiers to stop. The offended soldier cuffed him callously, and he fell to the ground. The youth got to his knees and begged, only to be met with a kick to his face.

Skarde growled, and his hand went for his sword. It wasn't there. He looked into the hut and saw the two scabbards on the ground where they had been dropped. Staggering over, he picked them up and strapped them on. Taking a deep breath, he steadied himself, and returned to the door. The boy and the old man were picking themselves and the pack up, and the gloating soldiers let them be at last. One of the soldiers looked his way.

Skarde ducked back into the hut. *I've overstayed my welcome!* There was no back entrance to the hut. Desperate, Skarde shuffled some of the supplies that line the wall opposite the door. He gave the wattle and daub structure a few solid kicks, opening just enough of a hole to crawl through. He scanned the hut for anything else of use. He grabbed three skins of water, but nothing else. *Fortune enough for a beggar*, he thought.

He crawled out of the hole and right away gripped his guts. He breathed deep and slow. Forcing himself forward, he crawled through tall grasses into a reedy ditch. He kept on, steady and silent until the contour of the jungle loomed before him. Skarde entered a thick cluster of trees and finally stood. He made little headway as he felt his way along. He was in dense undergrowth, and as the dawdling sun lit the sky, he was still within sight of the village. He crept along and at last came to another path. Here, his stomach grumbled.

"Bah, pain or hunger. Pick one," he chastised his gut.

Skarde moved away from the village with stealth. He soon came across a well-trod walking path. He stood for a moment to think; his mind was still swimming. He took a cautious drop from one of the water skins. It tasted clean, so he took a long draught. Right away, the pain in his gut came back, though less than before. He looked with yearning at the skin. The water was fulfilling but he would need to ration it. He mulled over his next steps. He would need to find food, a safe source of water, and a good place to hide for the night as he explored the island. *Escape from this cursed rock may come today*, he thought, *but more like it will be long and hard fought.*

To that point, he eyed the path he was on. Travel on a path might be perilous, there was a much greater chance of running into someone he'd rather avoid, but he had need to distance himself from the village. Some there did not appreciate his presence. The foliage however made for hard trekking. *I will march*, he thought, *'til noon along this path, then...*

He made off at a pace, but soon doubled over, his stomach heaving. With a burning throat, he rested his back against a tree and took another swig of water. *I must go slow*, he thought, his lips curled in a sneer. Illness was harder on his pride than his body. He moved along at a slower pace, his eyes searching constantly for food or foe. The sun rose higher in the sky, and on sudden, he came across six young men just out of boyhood. They sat in a green alcove ten feet from the main path and scarcely visible 'til he was right upon them. They looked at him with astonishment equal to his. Their eyes flickered over the giant Northman with no small hint of fear.

"Sahiyno!" they said among other words Skarde could not understand, staring wide-eyed at him.

They lowered their eyes in deference and offered up the food they carried. Skarde looked them over. They were not much of a threat. He saw they carried no weapons. Beside them, they had lain aside six light wooden frame backpacks with sacks of goods strapped to them. These were young men on their way to trade or perhaps offer tithe – not look for trouble.

"Share?" said Skarde pulling a water skin from his shoulder. He did not want to take food from them under threat of violence. The trade he offered was not fair, but it was a trade, and the chance at some food was too good to pass up. He crouched beside one who held up a rolled flat bread with what looked like goat cheese. He shook his water skin for him to take. The young man was confused. With caution, he extended a hand and took the skin as Skarde thrust it forward. Skarde took the rolled bread and signed a polite gesture. The young man dipped his head low. There was an awkward moment of glances.

They are waiting on me as a guest, he thought. He took a bite and the six young men smiled toothily and murmured approval as they again ate and drank. He wasted no time eating, then he said his thanks and rose to leave. They all raised their hands in salute, glad perhaps that he hadn't robbed or harmed them. Again, his guts felt as if they were filled with pins. He walked slowly and was glad, at least, his hunger abated. He felt as if he were carrying chains, though a few less than yesterday.

Suddenly, he cursed aloud at his lack of keenness as a soldier carrying a tangle of fine ropes in one hand and a spear in the other charged him. He drew a sword and slashed as the spearman tossed the net over him. It spread wide and lay over his sword arm. He pulled at the net, but the spearman charged him and thrust with his spear. Even partly restrained, Skarde was able to knock the shaft aside. He dived forward to attack, but he only deepened the hold of the net. The spearman retreated cautiously, keeping Skarde at bay. A realization flashed through Skarde's mind. *He but draws my attention!* Jumping away from the spearman, he pulled his arm free. He spun to run into the jungle afore his suspicion was proven, but it was too late. He caught sight of movement to the side of the trail and behind him came a small troop of men.

He sprang to the side and turned. The spearman hadn't attacked his back as he turned, but lunged forward now. He stabbed at Skarde, overly cautious. *He wishes to waste my time!* Skarde thought. He knocked the blow aside, his left hand shooting forward like a bolt to grab the spear. He yanked with a ferocious roar. Even ill, Skarde's strength was enough to put the spearman off balance. The spearman fought to wrest his weapon from Skarde's grasp, but right away Skarde hurled his great weight forward. The spearman toppled, and in a heartbeat, the tip of Skarde sword plunged into his throat with a crunch. Pulling his sword red tipped from his fallen foe, Skarde glanced from side to side. There were several soldiers running toward him down the path. Behind him, there were a few more.

He bellowed with a berserker light in his eye. "I will drag some of you to Hell with me!"

Skarde charged at those back along the path, and they halted in amazement: perhaps they had counted on him fleeing into the jungle. He saw that several carried cudgels and shields rather than swords. Three of those formed a line, and two with spears and nets fumbled through the dense undergrowth to flank him. He reached the line of cudgelmen before the spearmen got around him. He charged straight in, and they raised their shields. He turned at the last moment, leaping from a blow to the far side of his rightmost opponent. Skarde swung, but his stroke was batted aside by a well-timed cudgel and his upward stroke caught the edge of his foe's shield. Skarde reached out, gripped the rim and tore it aside. That turned away the downward cudgel-swing the warrior made just as Skarde stabbed at the guts of the warrior beside him. He struck deep and true. Blood wetted the ground as his foe uttered a horrifying croak.

Skarde stepped back and swung his sword at the spearman that got behind him now a moment too late; a net covered him and checked his swing. The spearman reversed his weapon and drove the haft of the spear into his stomach even as a cudgel battered his thigh. Skarde howled and cursed, and stabbed at the cudgelman, but his foe spun back untouched. Yet another net was tossed over him, and as he fought for space to stab one last time, his sword was battered with savage blows until even his iron grip failed.

Even in a red rage, his mind sought to answer a question: *why am I not dead? Why do they not stab me with a spear or hack at my limbs?* They grappled him. A dozen hands grabbed him, and three or four fists pummeled him. He reeled but stood as a rock against an ocean. His feet planted wide, his mightily thewed legs straining, his one free hand gripping and crushing the throat of one attacker among the swarm. With a choke, that one fell back coughing... now his free hand found itself on the pommel of a knife in his belt. Like a claw, it flicked out and was sheathed silently in a gullet. Copper smelling blood drenched Skarde's forearm. In shock, the mortally wounded man gripped his throat and staggered back. Hardly had he taken a step as Skarde's blade struck like a snake again in a flurry. Another fell bloody with three deep wounds in his side. A cudgel swung hard in to Skarde's gut. A lesser man might have been toppled or killed by such a blow, but Skarde's stomach was girded by cords of iron. Skarde jabbed quick left, leaving his attacker with a deep gash in his arm. He howled in pain and dropped his weapon. Skarde now felt a terrific blow behind his knees. His legs buckled, and he fell even as he lashed out with his knife. A man each restrained his hands, and as he struggled, the butt of a cudgel rammed his head. Pain and a flash of white light jolted through his skull. Then darkness.

Skarde awoke to a tremendous pain in his head. He fought the urge to wince. He opened one eye just a slit. He was somewhere dimly lit and cold stone cradled his back. He lay quiet, reaching out with his every sense. When he was sure he was alone, he opened his eyes and looked about. He was in a rough-hewn cell. There was only one solid wooden door with a two foot long slit at eye level. Beyond the slit, a wavering torchlight dimly lit Skarde's bare cell. He still wore his breeches and boots, but his weapons were gone. He sat up, his head reeling. He touched his temple and above it was a throbbing goose egg.

"Ha," he croaked. *A wonder my skull isn't cracked*, he thought in silence. *Nay, a wonder they did not slay me outright. Torture and revenge, likely.*

He stood.

His battered and bruised body groaned in pain, but he stood. He circled the small cell for no more reason but a stretch and the desire to move. He peered out the slit. Torchlight flickered from beyond a bend, but he could see no one and nothing of interest.

"Bah," he spat.

He paced 'til the kinks in his limbs straightened out.

I must have been carried here and ungently, he thought. He sat and pondered. He cursed himself and laughed at his folly.

Time dragged. He shut his eyes. *Might as well sleep.* Long hours passed. Soft footsteps wakened him. He cracked one eye open and watched the slit in the door darken. He kept still as a figure looked him over. The door opened and there was a ragged, nearly naked man in the door. Skarde feigned sleep as the man entered bearing a wooden plate and a cup. He had no weapon. He approached Skarde and left the meal by his feet.

"Don't you fear that I might kill you and make my escape?" Skarde said.

The man leapt up and clapped his hands.

"No," he said without fear but with a hint of laughter.

Skarde rose to rest on his elbow and looked at the man in surprise.

"It's no bones to me if you escape, but you won't get out running through that door. And as for death… I would like one last good fight," he said taking a step back and raising his hands for fisticuffs as a fighting man would.

Skarde laughed. Ragged and old as he looked, his pose was not that of a fool making a jape but that of a warrior. Skarde placed his accent as belonging to the distant tribes of the Northeast.

"Who are you?"

"I am Belgeti! Horselord. Golden Son… Slave."

Skarde looked him over wondering about his tale and his plight. "I believe you. You once had fortune and might? And fortune fell?"

"Yes," he said, standing tall and straight. "I had ten sons and daughters. I had a hundred horses. My spear was feared and my bow true. Long I rode with the wind in my hair!"

"What happened?" Skarde asked over the rumbling in his stomach.

Belgeti laughed sharply. "As you say... my fortune fell. I was cut down with my horse-brothers. Those of us that lived were sold into slavery. I was an ill-behaved underling and was beaten as often as I fought. I was bought and sold again and again and here I found myself. And you?"

Skarde sat up and took his cup in hand. He gave Belgeti an informal salute and guzzled it. "I got drunk in the wrong tavern."

Belgeti threw his head back in laughter. "If only we could drink together free and foolishly. We could cause some ruckus!"

Skarde laughed. "Did they send you here to cheer me up?"

"I would say not," Belgeti said. "I do not work at house duties. I work in the mine."

"To keep an eye on you?"

"Aye, and a lash," Belgeti said.

He turned about and in the dim light Skarde could see a hundred long scars.

"So why did they send you?"

Belgeti shrugged. "They say the Lord of the Isle is a wizard. They are strange. Who can say? Perhaps they send me to dishearten you and show that a warrior's virtues avail you nothing here."

Skarde stuck his fingers in the bowl of gruel and ate a mouthful. He swallowed the bland stuff without remark. "Would you fight them if you had a weapon and nothing but a chance in Hell?"

Belgeti grinned. "Yes."

"Then your spirit isn't broken, and I am heartened. They have made two mistakes."

Belgeti nodded with a smile. "I must go," he said ruefully.

As Belgeti turned and stepped out of the cell, Skarde called to him. "Belgeti. Should you escape, what would you do?"

He stood silent for a moment with a far-off look. His eyes spoke that he knew the answer but paused to savor the thought before speaking. "I will see my strong sons and swift daughters again. But not before I win a prize or two. Wind in your hair!"

Belgeti shut the door behind him with a thud. Skarde ate the tasteless gruel and drank his water with a somber heart, yet felt his strength renewed.

The cell was cruel confinement. Skarde paced back and forth. He was so restless to get out that he neglected to check his wounds, 'til at last a few aches caught his notice. His captors had treated him. Aside from a sore head and a few cuts and bruises, he was well. His arm had a new poultice and his guts no longer roiled. He looked through the thin window and neither saw nor heard anything of interest down the hall.

"Ho!" He yelled. "A-hey!"

The echo returned promptly. What stone prison he was in was not large. No one came to investigate the racket. At length, he pulled on the door. It was shut fast and solid as a rampart.

He sat again and let his mind wander. He imagined a younger Belgeti, riding the steppes. *What battle had gone ill for him? What treatment unfit for a warrior had he suffered at the hands of slavers?* He shuddered and his heart chilled.

"No!" He spoke to himself in the dim light.

His gaoler hoped to plant such grim thoughts. *But Belgeti was not broken, and I will not be either.*

Chapter Five

Not broken but frustrated, he shifted a dozen times and at last gave in to fitful sleep. He dreamt of riding beside many mighty but desperate warriors. They assaulted a wall manned by cruel defenders. Spears and arrows flew, and men died on both sides. Skarde dismounted his horse and climbed the wall as only a man of hill and mountain could. As he reached the top of the wall, it began to crumble. It was made of the stuff of shadows and illusion. He rode a great block in a tide of stone by will alone. All crumbled, leaving naught but a lonesome ruin. About him lay the dead. Attacker and defender, all of them slain or crushed. He stood alone, amid the destruction.

He awoke alone in the darkness with little to keep his mind off his hunger. Long hours passed and Skarde's heart beat hard in growing anger. He cursed both his captors and his drunken imprudence. He closed his eyes and daydreamed of past adventures and travels. Whatever course they set to drag his spirits, he would not follow. In that long silence, he felt a faint pulse in the hard stone. At first, he thought it was his heartbeat, but then he only just heard, as if from some huge distance, a deep pounding in the earth. It went on, a regular beat like a drum, then it ceased, only to start again. *Do I imagine a blacksmith hammering far below?* Skarde pondered it.

At long last, the door beyond his cell clanked open again. The sound of boots and rattling scale mail came to his ears. He remained seated this time and watched the shadows of at least two figures march by his door before the thin window was darkened. With a jangling of keys, the cell door swung open and an imposing man in armor holding an unsheathed sword stood in the door frame.

"Get up, dog."

Skarde looked him up and down and laughed.

"What cause have you for mirth?" The armored man said.

"One brave man you sent with naught but rags to bring my dinner. Now three, at least, have come armored and arms drawn to give me a walk?"

Skarde checked his tongue and did not outright call them cowards. He guessed they were constrained by their master not to do him harm, but they were warriors and warriors would be hard-pressed to let such an insult pass.

"Silence!" said the man in rage. "Dog, you will learn a civil tongue if you outlive the Master's wrath. Now rise and follow at my heel."

At leisure, Skarde stood and stared grimly at the warrior. "Lead on then."

The warrior scowled at the command and waved him on.

Skarde stepped through the open door. There were two spear men at his back and a second swordsman who walked ahead of the first. Skarde smiled. Though they were now cautious, and opportunities to cause trouble were doubtful, at least his pride was stoked in having four armed escorts.

The passages of the gaol were short but twisted, as if it had been cut from a natural passage. It met a larger way that extended fifty paces in either direction before curving out of sight. They took the path that leaned downward. Skarde felt an unease underground, and they were going deeper. They passed a few tunnels and chambers whose function he could not guess. At last, they stopped before a large double door wrought with fine metals. The lead guard commanded him to halt. The other warriors halted as well, several paces behind. As their clacking sandals and jangling armor quieted, Skarde could hear far off the sound of voices and the regular clang of hammers on steel, quicker and less weighty than the deep thunder he heard in his cell. He listened intently and swore he heard two, three, or perhaps more hammers and anvils.

They waited in silence as if expected. Skarde looked each of his guards in the eye and smiled.

"A private table, tavern keeper," he said.

"Silence!" The swordsman growled.

"Bah. I will not come here again."

The leader, moved to anger, took a step toward Skarde. At that moment, the great doors clacked and opened.

"Move!" the swordsman barked.

"Very rude," Skarde said, but he yielded. Now was a poor time for a fight.

The swordsman led Skarde, and the other guards followed behind. They came into a tall wide corridor. Upon his left and right were broad stairs that led up about eight feet and turned. The corridor went on a short way, its ceiling rising rapidly into a high natural dome hung with stalactites. Its floor was a large sand pit. As they entered, a murmur and growl echoed from the stone walls, and he heard a dozen threats uttered. Skarde found himself in a round arena or training floor; whatever its purpose, there were a hundred armed warriors jeering at him in the surrounding stone galleries illuminated by dozens of guttering torches. His eyes, now used to the subterranean gloom, winced at the brilliance.

Before and above him was a man Skarde took to be the master of this strange realm. Flanked by four men in impressive hauberks and capes was an august figure seated on a tall throne carved from stone. Alone among the angry throng, he sat silent and unmoved. Skarde set his eyes upon this man, heeding not the jeers of the crowd.

He sat confident on his throne; his body almost as muscled as Skarde's. His face older, yet timeless. Clean and unblemished was his tan skin. He wore a regal beard of black curls, and a black curled coif crowned dark eyes as unflinching as stone. A tall hat and a rich toga embroidered with gold was his raiment. Like a legendary king of the ancient world, Skarde beheld him... A figure more fit for tales of old than to be beheld by eyes of flesh.

Skarde was brought before him. He looked at the Master with blinking eyes. The soldiers kicked his legs out from behind him and threw him to his knees. The crowd erupted in a roar. Skarde struggled against many hands and nearly managed to rise when a spearman raised the butt of his weapon to strike him. Suddenly, they all froze, and the rowdy warriors silenced in a heartbeat. Skarde ceased his struggle and looked about. Their leader had raised a palm, and nothing else, neither word nor expression. A long moment passed, and perhaps satisfied at the return of order he lowered his hand.

The man to the Master's right, tall and powerfully built with peppered dark grey hair, clenched his jaw. As tense silence hung in the air, he locked eyes with Skarde and neither looked away.

At last, he spoke with a growl. "You. Filthy drunken barbarian of the North. You have slain nine of our men and injured four others. For what? How dare you!"

Skarde's eyes furrowed at the question. "For what? Why ask why a man eats? As for how I dare – as my people say, who dares... wins."

"The insolence!" The man barked. "I shall kill you now!"

He tromped down the stairs and from there, jumped to the pit floor.

"Hold, Tyhomir," spoke the seated figure.

The angered captain almost froze in place, his hand on his pommel.

"Does he not speak truth?" The seated figure said. His stony voice calm, yet it seemed to resonate about the arena.

Tyhomir breathed like a bull restrained. "Even primitive folk-wisdom may betimes hit the mark."

The seated figure sat watching for a long moment. "Speak your name, savage."

Skarde smiled at the chance to parley, but before a breath left his mouth his eyes caught an enchanting figure moving betwixt the pillars behind the Master's throne. She was naked save for a few baubles both savage and stately, which did naught for modesty but enhanced her charms. She was of a race Skarde had never seen, and young, though her gait and eyes spoke of long held confidence. Beautiful, she was. Skarde had seen more polished gems, but a sensuality seemed to rise from her like a steam. All eyes in the arena were on her, his included, save for the Master's. Yet Skarde noted that the Master's eyes glanced briefly in her direction before returning to their stony set. His lip curled ever so slightly in displeasure – the first crack in his stony mask Skarde had seen. Skarde smiled. He took his leisure and drank in the sight of her form.

"Skarde," he said, looking at her as she settled beside the seated figure, resting her thigh on upon the arm rest of the throne. She looked upon him more wolfishly than he looked upon her.

"A mercenary from the distant North," he added.

"How came you to escape my men?" he said.

"By their impatience," Skarde spoke without caution. A grumble arose in the crowd, but the Master silenced this with a sweeping glance.

"They unchained their captives two by two before fetters suitable for walking were fastened. A slow job. So, Captain Basan ordered more to be freed at once. Aye, a lucky stroke for myself and the dozen other fighting men captured in wicked Byzerdamen. With but a glance, we knew it was our chance. I struck the first blow and was half-way across the beach in a fool's heartbeat. As for the rest," he looked first at Tyhomir and then at the simmering mob of sharp eyes and clenched fists, "I slew many – I am sure Tyhomir's tally is sound – and made my escape with my own skill."

Tyhomir's eyes looked as if they alone could slay.

"Liar!" Boomed a voice from the gallery. "Basan did not falter. He escaped by some trick or deviltry!"

"Ha!" Skarde laughed. "'Tis you who are the liar! But why deny the good Captain's incompetence. By one fault or another of your own men, I still escaped!"

"Villain! I shall spill your guts!"

The incensed soldier pulled his weapon and stormed along the gallery toward the steps.

Again, the Master raised his hand. The man halted and the jeers of the crowd faded. "One accuses the other of lies and dishonor," he spoke. "Acerman, do you challenge this accusation."

"I do, my Lord!" Acerman said, only now mastering his rage.

"Skarde, will you retract your accusation or accept his challenge."

A duel. Perhaps my only and best chance... "Bah! I have slain nine. Why not ten?"

"Know that Acerman is my sword master. He is *mugal* and my undefeated champion."

"By my sword, I have lived. I won't cower so easily," Skarde said. "I accept!"

He shifted his gaze from the stone-faced lord to the naked girl, a twinkle in his eye. She held his gaze with ease. Her face remained aloof but for a slight up-turn of her lips. A dangerous smile that made Skarde's heart quicken.

"Then prepare yourselves. Northman, you may cleanse yourself and sleep in a private chamber. You shall face trial by combat tomorrow."

The Master neither spoke nor moved any further. Acerman nodded at his lord and coldly ignored Skarde. The guard pointed back the way he had come. They raised their weapons in threat but there was no need. Skarde glanced at the Master, smiled at the girl, and turned to stride back to the doors. In the main hall, the guards surrounded him, but the captain made a gesture, and they relaxed their weapons.

"I trust you won't do anything foolish. Lord Gul-Zagar has placed some value on you. It would be foolish to cross him now," he said to Skarde.

"Aye," Skarde said. "There is no need to fight you... not tonight at least."

"None the less, you will not be allowed to roam our halls free. I trust you not, barbarian. I will have an armed guard with you at all times. Come."

The guard captain led the group back along the corridors. "You'll be allowed to visit the baths to clean yourself up and then be shown to a private cell. Food will be brought to you."

"Roasted meat on the bone and ale, my good man," Skarde said.

"Ah," said the captain. "A display of that same wit that landed you here."

"Dried meat will do then."

Skarde smiled to himself if no one else would. Indeed, several scowled, displeased with his lack of respect for their leader. The dour group led him on until they reached a junction. There, they halted.

"Turze," said the captain to one of the guards.

"Yes, captain," he said.

"You've a quick blade. Any nonsense from the savage... spare no limb," the captain said to the swordsman. "And take him to the baths first. He stinks."

Turze nodded and the captain departed with his men. Skarde was left alone with the guard, who eyed him with disdain.

"Move," Turze said.

"I know not the way. Lead on," Skarde said with a wave of his arm.

"I'll not turn my back on you," Turze said darkly. He drew his sword and pointed the way.

"Hah!" Skarde laughed. He gave the guard a mocking bow and followed his point.

They travelled on through an underground labyrinth. Turze took a torch from a wall sconce before they walked almost a mile through tunnels of natural stone joined by carved tunnels, and blacker than night without the torch.

They crossed more than one fork, but Turze directed him with curt commands. Skarde was indeed tired, though he dared not show any sign of it to his enemy. Still, he kept track of where they were and where forks and junctures appeared. One passage had a scent of burnt iron. After that, he caught a faint whiff of acrid sweat and vomit... and realized it was his own self. He had been on long marches before, survived in the wilderness, and expected no regular baths. *By Thunir's girdle, that jungle has put a stink on me,* he lamented.

They turned into a tall, thin natural cavern with sloped sides. They walked along a narrow, chiseled pathway curving to the left. The air had become hot and humid, and ahead was a glow filtered through steam. They entered a large cavern lit by three odd glowing balls. Skarde's skin tingled. *Sorcery!* Turze did not seem at all concerned. The cavern ceiling dripped, and stalagmites and stalactites almost touched each other about the rim of the cave. The far half of the cavern was dominated by a pool large enough for a hundred men. It was unnaturally blue, and a faint metallic scent hung in the air.

"Well, stand not there gaping, savage," Turze said. "Get in and enjoy your last bath if indeed it is not also your first."

Skarde scoffed and turned toward the strange blue pool. The uncanny orb and waters sparked a deep unease in his barbarian soul, but he would not show it to his captors. He kicked off his boots, doffed his breeches and the loincloth underneath. He picked them up and strode to the pool.

"Ai!" Turze said. "Do not wash those filthy rags in the pool!"

Skarde ignored him and waded in. The rim of the pool was puddle deep and sloped slowly at first. Now, he could see that a dozen feet to his right there appeared a shelf like a bench under the surface. He waded over to it, and it was fully suited to sitting. It was not natural and running his hands over it, he could feel no mark of pickaxe or chisel. He sat and pondered this oddity as he scrubbed his clothes. As he did this, he instinctively looked about for his weapon... *it was taken, of course.* He shook his head.

"Hurry yourself," Turze commanded.

Skarde stood and wrung his clothes out. He made his way back to the gentle slope at the edge of the pool. He laid his breeches and loin cloth out, though in the steamy cave there was slim chance they might dry. Without regard for Turze, he waded back to the bench.

"You test my patience, barbarian," Turze said.

Skarde sat down and rested his back against the sloping cave wall. "I do," he said matter-of-factly.

Skarde soaked in the warmth of the water for a long while, his limbs aching pleasantly as they relaxed. He splashed the water over himself. Whatever these arrogant fools thought, he welcomed a good bath. He took his time and savored Turze's grumbles.

Presently, he had a queer feeling. He sensed that the very rock he sat on quivered. A slow grinding could be heard as if from far off. He looked at Turze, but the thug gave no hint that he heard or felt anything. He stood and took a step forward, looking for some sign. There was rippling in the surface of the water, and a few bubbles appeared in front of him. He took another step forward, his hackles raised. Abruptly, there was a tremendous whoosh and the surface of the pool erupted but fifteen feet from him.

"Gods!" Skarde swore. He leapt back on to the underwater bench and clung to the sides of the cave. Terrible heat washed over him, and steam filled the air. He covered his face, and in moments, the blast had been sapped of force and ended in a few great bubbles. Had he been closer to the boiling gout, he thought his flesh might be poached.

As the roar of the blast ebbed, Turze's laughter replaced it.

"You know about the geyser?" Skarde said.

"I do," Turze said with a sneer.

Skarde hopped back down into the pool. His scowl turned to a smile as he relaxed and thought of cracking Turze's neck. It was near silent. Besides the occasional drip and clink of Turze's armor, Skarde could hear the impatience in his breath. Then his keen ears heard the faint paddling of bare feet on stone. He turned his head and out of the shadows, the mysterious unclad girl appeared behind his guard. Turze hadn't heard her. She touched his arm and his head spun about as his hand flew to his sword.

She looked him square in the eye and waved her hand in the direction of the exit. He remained frozen, staring at her. Her gaze didn't waver. He glanced back at Skarde angrily and stomped off. Skarde smiled as she now looked at him. Alone with her, he did not hide his appreciation, brazenly gazing at her up and down. Still, he kept an ear out for the jangle of Turze's scale mail. It had ceased. Likely, he was awaiting outside the pool chamber.

She smiled at him and slinked to the edge of the pool. Muscles in her legs and stomach rippled as she moved. Her skin and face spoke of a soft life, but the steely thews beneath were more like a warrior's.

"Don't you fear the savage?" Skarde said. Her bravery struck him, and he thought of Belgeti.

Her eyes flashed. Was danger a thrill for her?

"Would you take me by force, savage?" She said, stepping deeper into the pool. Her eyes held his, and he could feel his pulse quicken. "Would you murder a maiden? Or take me as hostage?" She stood before him but a step away, her hands defiantly on her hips and her charms openly displayed.

Skarde smiled. He took in her features. *From what far off region of the world does she hail?* "Are all your people so brazen?"

"No. They are modest and dull," she said.

"Why have you come," he asked.

"For pleasures of the flesh," she said.

Skarde laughed even as he eyed her wolfishly. "Girl! You are as blunt as you are shameless."

"Your tongue is silvered neither. You are a man of action, are you not?"

"Aye, girl. But will not your Master have both our heads on boards?"

"I am not his queen nor his concubine. I do as I please. As for your worries... most like you will be dead tomorrow."

Skarde looked at her, bewildered. *Perhaps, by her physique, she is a warrior*, Skarde thought, *an assassin? Too young to be a counselor. A hostage? A royal ward?* She lifted her leg and slid her foot over his thigh, and fire ran through his veins.

"Who are you?" Skarde asked.

"Sulmei," she said. "Do I not please you?"

"Most pleased, but you leave me thunderstruck."

"And I may do so again."

Skarde grinned and leaned forward to grab her by her rump. He pulled her onto his lap, and she tossed her hair back with a laugh. She kissed him before he could say anymore, and their natural bent led them on. They tested each other in rough passions. The night deepened, but neither player's lust dulled.

"You have been an admirable lover, barbarian," she said at last. "These men here are haughty and inattentive. Alas, I must go."

Skarde smiled. "I have never met a lass as bold."

"Farewell, Skarde," she said standing in the pool. "Die a good death tomorrow."

"How can you be sure it is I who will die?"

"Acerman is *mugal*. Gul-Zagar's sword-master, who teaches the men in the warrior's arts," Sulmei said.

"Fighting isn't about fancy swordplay, girl. It's about winning," Skarde huffed.

"Doubtless. But Acerman is renowned for his skill and his stoic mettle. He picks the mightiest opponents apart with cunning."

"Stoic? That mad-eyed spittle flinger? Do we speak of the same man?" Skarde eyed bubbles brewing where last the hot blast had blown. "Take care, Sulmei. The geyser."

"You have uniquely provoked him," she said backing away from him.

"Bah! He is hardly unflappable if one insult unhorses him," he said, eyeing the unsettled water.

"Challenging a man's reputation before his peers brings out a man's heat," she said. "But you have done him an injury a thousand-fold more egregious."

"How so?" *Is she unaware of the danger?* The water gurgled menacingly. He stood and shouted, "Girl, move!"

"... look to his eyes for the answer."

The water exploded and a scalding wave of heat roared over him. He sat back on the bench and covered his face with his arm. The steam was hotter than before, and it had only begun to wane when he surged forward, thrashing at the water to find her.

"Sulmei! Sulmei!" he bellowed, pushing quickly through the pool.

He found the ragged, semi-circular vent from which the geyser erupted, but Sulmei's body was nowhere to be found.

"Thunir!" Skarde swore. He wondered what had happened to her.

He looked around the cave, searching in the weird orb-light for anything he might have missed, but nothing was laid bare. Her uncanny disappearance made him feel uneasy. The unnatural gleam of the light globes even more so.

"Why couldn't I have been seized by normal slavers?"

Skarde dunked himself one last time and left the pool. He shook himself off as best he could. His clothes were roughly as wet as they were when he laid them out, so he wrapped on his loincloth and carried his breeches. He left the cave of the pool and found the tunnel pitch black. He shrugged, and continued on his way, trusting his memory. The thought of finding his way out and making an escape crossed his mind, but he dismissed it. A swarm of warriors who knew the terrain could be sent after him, and if he were stuck on an island as he thought, his cause would be lost. *I stay and fight.* Hardly had he decided this before his eyes made out a faint flicker ahead of him. He had made his way slowly in the dark but felt there should be a side tunnel nearby. He found it with ease and waited there. He crouched down out of sight. Most likely, it was the guard coming to retrieve him, but he did not know or trust these blackened tunnels, and his encounter with Sulmei had placed even more doubts in his mind. Faint footsteps grew nearer, and the light grew. Again, his hand sought a blade, and his lip curled as he found none. Whomever it was, he was close, and Skarde readied himself to lunge if needed. The light flared, and indeed, it was the guardsman come back with a fresh torch.

"Turze!" Skarde shouted as he stood.

Turze jumped and spun about, his sword out and a look of shock on his face. Skarde was glad he kept a dozen feet back.

"Barbarian!" Turze yelled, his eyes bulging. "Curse you, you damn fool! I should cut you down where you stand!"

"Turze, my friend, I came halfway back through this pitch-black maze to save you the trouble and you greet me like this?

"Do..." he said, mastering his anger. "Do not jest with me! Now move."

Turze jabbed his sword down the tunnel from where he had come. Skarde grinned, tossed his breeches over his shoulder, and stepped proudly. Turze's scale mail rattled more than it did on their outward journey, and he breathed heavy.

"You have wasted a great deal of time. I had to race back along these tunnels to refresh my torch and return hence as you dallied," he growled.

"Good to know! A fireside tale for a skald!" Skarde said, one of the few ironic sayings among his grim people, and thus one of his favorites.

Turze grunted through his teeth and said no more. Skarde thought of Sulmei and her pleasant company, but also on what she had said and the manner of her disappearance. *Look to his eyes,* she had said. Skarde wondered what she meant. *And why would she come to give me advice?* He had more questions than answers. As they found their way into larger ways, and their walk came to an end, he almost asked Turze about Sulmei. He thought asking a foe for knowledge as foolish as complaining about one's feet. But Turze offered up some of his own advice unbidden.

"Don't be too pleased with yourself. You are far from the first to enjoy her charms, or the last. She is a witch. You are but her plaything – or a tool," he said.

Skarde smelled some jealousy on his breath, if not fear.

Skarde spoke not for a moment. Sharp words came to him with ease. He felt there was fire here, and he spoke a little more softly, if not with craft. "Who is she?"

"As I said, a witch and a whore." He spoke with rancor. "The Master alone knows what purpose she serves, other than to placate the men... or stir them into conflict. You are but a momentary fancy."

Skarde listened and took in the words. *A witch? Perhaps that's how she escaped the geyser... but why her interest in me?*

Turze sneered, enjoying the bafflement in Skarde's eyes. "Here is your cell," he said waving his hand at a simple but sturdy looking door.

Skarde roused from his thoughts. He strode to the door and opened it. Inside was nothing but a rude cot, a jug, lantern, tinderbox, and a chamber pot.

"Enjoy your last..." Turze said.

Skarde stepped into his cell and shut the door before Turze could finish speaking.

Chapter Six

Skarde slept well enough for a man about to die. He awoke in darkness to a shuffling outside his door. That was followed by the clack of armor, and the faint light of a torch under the crack. He felt about for the tinderbox on the small table beside him and lit the lantern. Standing, he stretched as he dawdled to the door stark naked. He opened it and was met by a figure in the dim light. The figure moved back and laid a hand on the sword pommel at his belt. *Another guard to keep me company*, he laughed to himself. On the ground near the post of the door was a bowl of boiled grains and meat, and a wooden pitcher. Skarde smiled toothily at the guard and picked up the meal. Slamming the door, he hungrily ate the food, glad for a bit of meat, and drained the weak wine in the pitcher. He donned his loin cloth and threw himself back into the bed.

Fast broken, and nothing to wait for but death, Skarde sat and wondered about who Sulmei was. What did she want with him? It could have been pleasure, as she claimed, but her parting words were guidance.

"She wants me to live," he whispered to himself, weighing his own words. "Why? Because I am handsome? True," he nodded sagely. "Out of kindness? And watch her fellow die? Does she plot against him? Perhaps she is a jilted lover?"

Skarde thought of Turze's accusation that she was a woman of wanton spirit. "Well, perhaps Acerman is the jilted lover… and a threat?"

There was a robust knock at the door, and it swung open before Skarde had a chance to respond. It was another guard, an officer by the high-handed look about him.

"Come, barbarian. Time for your trial," he spoke.

"At last," Skarde said. "I was tiring of the gossip."

The guard looked at him as if he were mad. He bounded out of the bed and approached the door.

The officer eyed his near nudity with disdain. "Don your breeches, man."

"Before we go, I must ask – will my opponent be wearing armor?"

"If he wishes, he will be," the officer said.

"And am I to be given armor?" Skarde asked.

The guard laughed. "Ha! Of course not."

Skarde looked at the simple, still damp looking leather breeches. "Then, I go as I am. I don't need the frippery."

The officer shook his head and waved him forward. He stood back and Skarde strode out into the dismal tunnels. Skarde knew the way and marched slowly, stretching his limbs to ready himself for a fight. He led him straight back to the arena. There, he was marched without delay through the great doors. Ahead, he caught sight of Gul-Zagar on his throne, noble and unmoving. He was exactly as he appeared yesterday, as if he had truly turned to stone and just now back to flesh again. On the dais by his feet, lounging upon silken throws and pillows, was Sulmei. As naked as yesterday, she wore only jewel-bedecked splendors; dainty ceremonial silver greaves, bracers, and a silver tiara wreathed by a fan of peacock feathers. Her face painted in thin black lines and dots in a manner he had never seen before. She seemed an uncanny, decadent figure out of place amongst the sober martial surroundings. As he entered the arena, a wall of warriors in the stands jeered and pounded their armor. As the noise rose to a cacophony, Skarde looked about.

"Thunir!" he swore under his breath.

The arena was packed with soldiers. Skarde guessed a thousand in number, matching what his pursuers in the jungle had boasted. They had all come for the spectacle of the duel and to witness their fellow's revenge upon him. They all wore not the practical garb of sailing and fighting, but uniforms of red tabards emblazoned with the device of a silver sword, and black cloaks.

"They are an army!" He gasped.

These are no mere pirates, he thought. *Who is this Gul-Zagar to gather a force like this on some nameless island? Here is Acerman... my questions must wait...*

His foe strode forward through the archway opposite him, a young soldier at his side. The jeers of the host turned to cheers, and they stamped their feet like thunder. Skarde noted that he, indeed, wore armor. The same fine scale mail as he wore yesterday. He carried an unsheathed sword in his right hand, and a long, thin dagger hung at his belt. His eyes were almost as stony as Gul-Zagar's, his face calm but resolute. Acerman gestured at the young soldier behind him, and he strode forward.

In his hands were two scabbards. In his left was a spotless and new scabbard of the kind the brotherhood carried. In it was, no doubt, one of their finely crafted swords. In his right was a battered and road-worn scabbard – and quite familiar. Skarde's eyes widened as did his smile. It was his own sword, taken when he was captured. Though it was notched and well used, it was his, and it fit his hand like a glove. He laughed in joy, stepped toward the young man, and took hold of his old blade. Skarde unsheathed it, twirled it in the air and grabbed its hilt in mid-air.

"My thanks!" Skarde said.

The young man sneered and walked out of the arena. Acerman walked around to Skarde's side, keeping a good ten sword lengths away and turned toward Gul-Zagar. Beside the master of the isle stood Tyhomir, who stepped forward to address them.

"Selamah and honor, warriors!" Tyhomir bellowed in the Sharoshan tongue. "By judgement of the Master's wisdom, this outlander, Skarde by name, has been granted right of combat…"

The warriors in the stadium grumbled, though not loudly, as if loath to challenge their leader.

Tyhomir smiled at this. "For the barbarian's foul accusations, our Acerman..."

The crowd suddenly exploded with noise, chanting, and beating their fists against their mailed chests. Skarde looked to Gul-Zagar. He remained stock still, his face remained a stoic mask. Whatever control he exerted over these warriors, he gave them leeway to vent. Sulmei, on the other hand, was not so detached. She scanned the crowd and put on a lofty air, but Skarde could sense a glint of dread in her eyes.

"Our Acerman, Brother and Mugal of the Sword, challenges these lies, these insults! They duel to the death!"

Again, the crowd roared. Tyhomir drew his sword, held it high, and yelled above the din. "Fight!"

Skarde bellowed and bounded at Acerman.

He swung his sword down at Acerman's head. Acerman deftly stepped to the side, his sword on high guard, and he swung back at Skarde. Skarde had not expected to kill his foe so easily. He more desired to show that he was not cowed by talk of Acerman's skill, and the thunderous chants of the hostile audience. Expecting a riposte, Skarde dodged aside, yet Acerman's blade came deadly close to his unarmored stomach. Smoothly recovered, Acerman's blade came thrusting quick as a snake at him, and though Skarde parried it and swung back, his attack fell wide.

"Curse of P'thon!" Skarde swore.

Acerman's frigid expression broke with the hint of a curled lip. Now, with that hint of cruelty, his face took on a familiar hue. He came on with cold aggression and knocked Skarde's sword aside. Only Skarde's lightening reflexes saved him from a hacked limb. Skarde came back with several deft thrusts and swings, one after the other. He had hoped to use his greater size and longer sword to advantage, but he landed no blow. Acerman was bold, trusting, correctly, that his armor would protect him from all but the most well-placed strikes. Skarde kept on the offense, moving in and out, and hoping to force Acerman to move in his heavy scale mail as much as himself in but a loincloth. Acerman took no bait and fell for no feint.

"Are you ready to die?" Acerman said with a sneer.

His sneer highlighted his high cheekbones and his piercing blue eyes. *The eyes!* Skarde was struck with the sudden realization that Acerman was the brother of Captain Basan. He backed off a pace to give himself a moment. *Thunir! Sulmei must be testing me, or she would have spoken more plainly. I will break his frosty demeanor. Now, mayhap, my sharp tongue will dig me out of a hole instead of into one.*

"Aye, after watching your brother die like a coward. What more merriment could I want!"

"He died bravely in battle," Acerman said with cold fury.

"If that is what you call it. He was brave enough when he thought to carve up my back. Not so when I turned to face him," Skarde said his voice thick with mockery.

"Liar!" Acerman spat, striking at Skarde's head as if to silence him.

Skarde knocked the blow away.

"How he wept when he faced me. No warrior, he! My sword went through his guts, and he bawled!" *How did the children of the South call for their mothers?* "Amma! Amma, he bawled like a child. Oh, help me!"

"Liar, he fought as bravely as I do!" Acerman yelled,

"Nay, you are braver than he. You look into my eyes, at least... though you fight in armor and with your fellows all about, and I fight naked and alone. Braver than your wallowing brother! Waaah!"

Skarde got his wish. Acerman roared and struck again and again with a fury. Skarde retreated, step by step, defending himself from one swift and near-true strike after another. Acerman nearly bested him more than once, and only his wildcat-like reflexes and warrior's instincts saved him.

"Thunir!" Skarde swore. *The witch's advice will be the death of me!*

He sprang back and glanced up at the dais for a flashing moment. Sulmei was now up on her knees, as if ready to fly into the action, her eyes wide with alarm. Bullheaded, Acerman was upon him again.

I will not win this fight with sword-skill, Skarde realized, *but...*

As he clashed with Acerman, they came into a close bind. Fast as a whip, Acerman reversed his stroke, but Skarde predicted it and caught his foe's pommel in both hands... by dropping his own sword! Acerman's eyes went wide, but he pulled his stroke high in a flash to free himself from Skarde's grasp. Rather than striking Acerman's exposed face, Skarde stepped in, quick as a bolt, and grabbed his foe's pommel. Acerman growled in annoyance and twisted the blade down hard and fast. Had Skarde not been so strong, he might have lost control and been cut to ribbons. As it was, the blade cut his arm. But at last, he could bring his weight down on Acerman.

He threw his elbow high and came down with a crushing blow upon Acerman's grip, and they both lost a hold on the sword. Without missing a beat, Acerman threw a mailed fist into Skarde's jaw. It was a staggering blow, but Skarde growled like a mad animal and threw a wild flurry of punches. He knew if he backed off for even a moment, Acerman would likely take back his sword and death would swiftly follow. Acerman ducked low, hoping his mailed shoulders would take some of Skarde's fury, and as he came up, he brandished his dagger.

Sulmei, unseen by Skarde, gasped and turned her head away.

By luck or his wild-man's reflexes Skarde caught his wrist, and a deadly contest for control of the blade took place. He held Acerman with both hands, and Acerman fought back alike. Acerman was strong, but Skarde was stronger. Inch by trembling inch, the point of the blade turned in toward Acerman's guts, and with a grim smile, Skarde pressed it in. The point caught on his foe's scale mail. Skarde rammed a thunderous knee kick to drive the blade home, but Acerman shoved it downward, and that blade also fell to the sandy ground.

Acerman recovered expertly, and twisting, brought a mailed hook to Skarde's head. Skarde felt rather than saw the blow coming, and himself twisted out of the way, only to take the fist on his wounded arm.

"Ahhg!" Skarde bellowed. Fury ran red through his veins.

He threw a punch with his good arm, but it didn't connect. He brought his injured arm up, now burning, bloody, and sluggish to ward off another attack from Acerman. Skarde took a booted foot in his stomach and was thrown back, gasping. He grunted and squared off with Acerman. Frustrated, Skarde found his opponent's skill at brawling was equal to his skill with the sword. Still, there was a desperate light in Acerman's eye. *He's tiring*, Skarde thought.

Skarde rushed him, and Acerman threw expert blows, rolling away from him. But Skarde had the greater reach, greater power, and the mad endurance of a berserker. He threw wild blow after wild blow before recklessly seizing Acerman's tabard and delivering a savage headbutt. Blood spattered Skarde's face, and Acerman staggered. Like a battering ram, Skarde pummeled him relentlessly, abandoning the art of the duel for brutality. Acerman fell and hit the ground like a sack. Hardly had he hit the sand as Skarde stomped upon his throat with his bare heel. Something snapped, and Acerman's head turned at an unnatural angle.

The uproar of the crowd was strangled in an instant, and Skarde stood before them covered in blood, his chest pounding deep and steady like bellows. Sulmei looked on in blanched horror, her face as vivid as Gul-Zagar's was unmoved.

"Our Mugal!" cried one warrior.

"Kill him! Kill the *gavirh*!" another shouted.

In moments, eight of the warriors had vaulted from their stone perch to the sandy floor and drew their swords. Teeth clenched, Skarde scrambled to pick up his sword. With a dire glint in his eyes, he turned to face them. Suddenly, the sand of the gladiatorum floor surged up, and formed what looked like a giant palm. The pale-yellow hand slammed into the charging warriors and hurled them fifteen feet, knocking them to the ground. As they groaned and struggled to rise from the crashing blow, sand pouring from their bodies, Skarde glanced at Gul-Zagar. He stood and his palm was still raised before him, his face as stony as ever.

"Sorcery!" Skarde whispered hoarsely to himself.

"Skarde has bested Acerman," Gul-Zagar spoke, his voice carrying its weight to every corner of the arena. "He has crossed the Bridge of Death, and by right of triumph earned a place among us, if he so chooses."

All eyes settled upon him. He looked about and saw their pain and hate, and marveled how Gul-Zagar kept them so, like dogs on a leash.

"Aye. I will take my place among you," he said, not doubting that any other words would bring a swift death.

"Then sheathe your swords, O Iron Brotherhood. Raise your fist beside your brothers. Stand eternally proud," Gul-Zagar's voice rang out, like stark military music.

They did as they were told right away. They sheathed their swords, pounded their chests, and held their fists up, though their faces fumed with smoldering animosity. The thousand soldiers about the arena did the same.

Gul-Zagar turned and stared at Tyhomir for a moment before clapping him roughly on the shoulder. Tyhomir bowed his head in deference, and Gul-Zagar strode away with unhurried pomp. Sulmei had recovered, and she stood and sauntered over to Tyhomir's side. Her chest rose and fell deeply as she breathed deep, and looked upon him and those in the arena with worried eyes.

"You may choose your weapon, O brother" Tyhomir spoke to him coolly, gesturing at the blades strewn about the arena.

"My sword has never failed me. I will trust to it," he said, picking up his old sword.

Those warriors in the pit approached the body of Acerman. One pulled his cloak off and laid it carefully beside the body.

With care, he and two others lifted the corpse and laid him gently upon it.

"Toran," Tyhomir called out.

"Before Acerman's spirit departs, I would have him know that I choose you to be Mugal."

Toran looked woefully at Acerman's broken body.

"I have not earned the right," Toran said.

"You have. You were his best pupil and taught many alongside him. You are Mugal," Tyhomir said.

"I will do what I can, though I am not his equal," Toran said, his voice breaking.

"You are Mugal," Tyhomir said. "Now, take our brother's body to the Apothecary-Priest."

Skarde stood aside, sheathing his sword. He remained silent. Toran, and five others carried Acerman out the door. He could have forgotten that a thousand pairs of eyes watched the same procession, so still were they. At last, he turned his eyes back toward the dais. Sulmei was gone. Tyhomir stood looking at him coldly.

"Clean yourself up, and return to your cell," he said.

His arm still bled and began to pain him. Skarde took a deep breath, and left, seeking no help from anyone.

He found his way back to his little room, avoiding Acerman's procession to the Apothecary-Priest, though to a healer is where he should have gone. He would not chance being about Toran and his mourning fellows yet. Gul-Zagar seemed to have tremendous influence over the warriors, but if he were in Toran's place, revenge would be heavy on his mind. He dabbed the stinging flesh of his arm clean as best he could and cast about for some way to close the wound. He tore a piece of cloth from his blanket and wrapped it about his arm. Then he lay back to rest as his overburdened body yearned for. He drifted into a half sleep, thinking it best to stay put 'til tempers cooled. *Revenge will come upon me a-time, by one doom or another. I must get off this island. Besides, there are no taverns.*

Hours had passed, and half in a dream, Skarde saw his door press open a crack. Skarde's hand found the familiar pommel of his old sword. He snapped to attention, ready to pounce, though he lay perfectly quiet. The form in the opening door frame looked familiar.

"Belgeti?" Skarde said.

"Aye. I've come to battle to the death," he said, holding up a pouch. "I would have come sooner, but these damn caves... a poor swap for open sky."

Skarde sat up, his arm groaning in pain. "Welcome, friend. But I am sad to say I am half dead already."

"Lucky," Belgeti said coming in. "If I were half dead, maybe I'd get to lay down." He laughed at his own joke, and Skarde smiled. "Peg-Leg sent me."

Belgeti sat on the stool nearby Skarde's bed and began opening the pouch. He glanced at Skarde's arm as he pulled bandages and a smaller pack out.

"How did you survive this long taking care of cuts like that?" he said.

Skarde shrugged and winced at the growing pain. "Wine and luck."

Belgeti laughed and began undoing Skarde's crude bandage.

"Who is Peg-Leg? A guard?" Skarde asked.

"Yes," Belgeti said. "I don't know his name. All guards in the mines have names like that. Burned-Man. Grim-Face. I don't know their real names."

"Did he send you the first time?" Skarde asked.

"Yes," Belgeti said. "He sent me to serve you supper in gaol. He's nice enough for a guard."

"Hmm," Skarde said, wondering fruitlessly for the moment about this guard.

Belgeti had a roll of fresh cloth out and a thick unguent that smelled of spices. With no warning, he slathered the stuff into Skarde's wound. Skarde's jaw stiffened, and he let out a quiet but strained breath.

"Ah... it tickles?" Belgeti said.

Skarde gave him a rictus grin.

"You'll have a lovely scar in a few weeks. Who gave you this scratch?"

"Acerman," Skarde said. "He was unhappy with me."

Belgeti leaned back to look at Skarde in surprise. "Acerman? Is he still unhappy?"

"No," Skarde said. "He is dead."

"Ohh! Chu-chu-chu!" Belgeti cackled, eyes wide. "Now scream."

"What? Ahhh!" Skarde grunted as Belgeti jabbed him with a bone needle strung with catgut.

He gritted his teeth again as pain struck him silent. Belgeti also was silent, steady upon his work, allowing Skarde to ponder why the stitch was always more painful than the blade. At last, he bit down on the thread, and wound a clean cloth about his arm.

"Best to work fast when you have no wine," Belgeti said.

"For you or me?"

"For me."

Skarde laughed. He tested his arm with slow movements.

Chapter Seven

Skarde missed Belgeti's company as time passed, for Belgeti's place was in the mines. None spoke to him, though he was left water and food. Skarde had spent, a-times, long lonesome moons with naught but his own thoughts to keep him. Those times chafed him, but he walked free. The walls of stone about him became as a suffocating tomb. He wandered the endless tunnels, but they did not satisfy. He learned their paths, though some places he could not go. At length, he came to the mouth of this underground Hell. Guards and an iron gate blocked his path.

"Let me up, so I might see the damned sky!" he said, but they withheld him.

Perhaps, he mused, *Belgeti and I can hatch a plot to escape and ride over the ocean, if he truly be a lord of horses.*

He rested. He was fed. He healed, and he was bored. He laughed in scorn when a swordsman came to him and was told he would be trained with a batch of recruits. In truth his heart swelled at the idea.

He was moved from his cell into a room of bare stone walls. There were forty simple beds aligned in four rows, and twenty-five men joined him, all rough looking and battle scarred. One of the swordsmen directed the men with terse shouts as Tyhomir oversaw. These, as Skarde learned, were recruits to whatever be the cause of the Master. These were now his quarters. These now his mates, and with them, he would train.

Skarde's heart shifted between a desire to fight, even if just in practice, and the slight to his pride at being trained. When Tyhomir commanded them, his face soured at the idea. Tyhomir's eyes would turn in his direction and await an open challenge. They were to leave their earthly possessions in rough-hewn but expertly made boxes at the feet of their beds, and they were led out for training. Skarde's spirit rose somewhat. He had fellows, strangers though they be, and a purpose, though it not be his. *This is better than being dead or a slave*, he thought.

They entered the arena once more and lined up in soldierly fashion. The place was dark, and Tyhomir alone carried a torch, a beacon leading the way. He stood still, grim faced, and watching over them. The moment wore on, but none spoke out or dared to challenge the solemnity in the air.

Skarde's eyes widened as flames suddenly flared in two brass braziers set upon the center stage. The dignified and ominous form of Gul-Zagar was outlined with red and shadow as he ascended with pomp to stand before the assembled men. Behind him came Sulmei, like a glass figure limned in dancing light, who wore nothing but a ruby studded diadem of brass which bore enormous, curved horns, brass greaves, and wicked looking brass vambraces which bore long whip-like spikes. Despite her brazen beauty and fantastical appearance, the eyes of the men were drawn to Gul-Zagar, a figure of awe and dread.

No eye could look away, and Skarde's spirit chafed at the sudden feeling of insignificance. His breath quickened as drums thrummed, and The Master spoke. His voice was deep and sonorous, and was heard, somehow, more from within Skarde's own head than with his ears. He was drawn by the power and wisdom of Gul-Zagar's words, though afterwards, he could recall only glimmers of what was spoken. Some of those glimmers the Master spoke of was chaos and the folly of men, and Skarde was ashamed. He spoke of doom and destiny. There they were, on the cusp of ruin, of barbarism and eternal darkness, and they were there to answer a call. His spirit lifted. They were brothers and heroes against the darkness. They would fight and be kings of men. Even in death they would triumph.

Skarde's heart swelled with nobility and zeal. He sought adventure and glory, and here it was in ample supply if he chose. *If I chose*, he thought. Yet now it seemed to him that his eyes were held, and his mind drawn along subtly but inescapably. He hadn't noticed the sway 'til the thought of choice came into his mind. Just the thought of turning away now was difficult, and as he set his thought at it, it seemed as if he had turned from floating along with a powerful river to swim against the torrent.

I will choose. He gritted his teeth. It was a physical effort. He could not draw his eyes away from the figure of Gul-Zagar. *I... I must be free...* With sweat on his brow, he turned and looked at the profile of a face two men away. He looked like an older mercenary he had briefly known a year ago. A loud braggart whose tales far exceeded his everyday appearance. With that laughable braggart in mind, he breathed and shook the glamour from his head.

He had fought against a torrential river, and now was washed ashore. Exhausted and breathing deep, he could still hear The Master. His voice was majestic, his words profound, but Skarde could shake away their power. He dared to lift his face and look about, though he kept his gaze from landing directly on Gul-Zagar. All, it seemed, but him were rapt at attention, awe struck, and eager.

"Funir's wing!" he muttered under his breath. "They are all ensorcelled."

His gaze wandered forward and fell upon Sulmei. Her face was near as stonelike as The Master's, but Skarde saw a twinkle, and knew she was glancing at him. There was the slightest curl of a smile upon her lips, and then her gaze turned as if she hadn't noticed him.

She knows I have resisted Gul-Zagar's charm. Is she pleased? His spine tingled. A word from her might mean death. He kept his face forward and let his eyes bore into the back of the man's skull before him. At last, The Master's sermon came to an end. The men raised their fists and their voices in thunder, and Skarde did the same, and felt much the same quickening in his blood.

"Hodan and Thunir," he muttered under his breath. "What have I gotten myself into?"

Skarde was now taken and placed with the others in the barracks. He was permitted to keep his sword beneath his bunk, but not to carry it. He chaffed at this, and at the wooden sword he was given, but in a rare moment held his tongue. All were given new clothes which he took with a smile. His old breeches and loin cloth were foul rags after long trials and his boots were tattered.

Freshly arrayed, they were marched off for training. There, Toran and another swordsman – Toran's newly chosen protégé Skarde thought – awaited their entry and good order. As they arranged themselves, Skarde bounced on his heels and twirled his stick... and noted he was perhaps a pace or so away from where he had slain Acerman.

"Ha. And now the student will teach me," he spoke to his new compatriot beside him, though they had scant time for talk.

His legs were restless. Though he hardly had enough time to recover from illness and injury, his iron constitution staved off exhaustion. Though friendly enough, the man he had spoken to did not reply but kept his attention forward. Like the rest of the men, Gul-Zagar's spell, if that be what it was, lay on him and he was wide-eyed in earnest.

"Be still!" Toran bellowed. "Though ye be fighting men one and all, ye fight now not for mere riches but for the glory of the Iron Brotherhood. For the ordering of the world! You shall wear the finest steel upon your breast and wield a sword made for a king! But you must earn it!" he said with a dire drop in his voice.

Skarde gasped and reeled back as if he were reacting to the overdone melodrama of a tavern storyteller.

Toran stared coldly at him. "Some of you shall be undone by your arrogance. But fools themselves may serve as examples for others."

"Speak for yourself, man," Skarde said unable to bridle his tongue any further.

"And the fool speaks on command!" Toran said swinging his wooden sword about.

Skarde scoffed. "You know as well as your master that I need no training."

A sneer passed over Toran's face and Skarde wondered if he had pressed his luck too far. Toran stood stock still, and after a few heartbeats of tense silence, he pointed his wooden sword at four men.

"You four, stand beside me," he said. "And you," he jabbed his sword at four others. "Stand beside Skarde, over there."

The four looked apprehensively at each other, and with displeasure at Skarde. Skarde shrugged and strode to the spot

Toran had pointed out. Toran and his men stood in a circle murmuring. Skarde's proscribed allies turned to him and awaited his direction with raised brows.

"A contest," Skarde said. "Stick together and work as one."

They nodded, dubious but united.

"Here is your task," Toran said. "Simply throw us five down any way you can. Our goal is the same. When a man is off his feet, he stays down. Begin!"

Skarde thought some contest of this sort was planned. He right away howled a war cry and charged in. He menaced Toran, but jumped aside at the last moment and hacked down with his wooden sword at the warrior to his left. The man was almost taken unawares but raised his weapon in a counterstroke as he leapt back. Toran was on him right away, and Skarde was hard put to counter. His mates circled just as Toran's crew came at him, and just in time. He retreated a step and fell in with the rest in a battle line. In a flurry of blows bruises were exchanged, and both gangs fell into a defensive posture. Everyone pulled a half step back. With swords up, and stances wary, Skarde readied to pounce forward. He was impatient to knock at least one foe down. Before he could, Toran barked a command. Two men at his left slid around behind Skarde.

Skarde roared and slashed at Toran.

Emboldened, his mates circled and struck out at Toran. He was ready for it and knocked aside or dodged every attack. Skilled as he was, he could not stand long against three. Skarde growled, eager to take Toran down, but Toran let out a cruel laugh. The two men who had run around Toran had overwhelmed the furthest left of Skarde's men. Knocked over, he stumbled headlong into Skarde's legs.

"Hells!" Skarde spat, just as Toran's wooden sword thrust past his chin.

He had barely dodged the tip. He bounded back and quickly took stock of the situation. One man was down and dazed, and another put up a frenzied guard. Toran stepped to the side and slashed at another, putting him off balance. Two of Toran's men rushed to take his place and Skarde warded off a fury of blows.

Toran, with some flair, stepped to the side of his opponent and slashed high. It was a ruse, and he kicked at the man's knees, toppling him.

"Thunir!" Skarde roared, and he launched himself at his closest foe.

He knocked a blow aside and slammed a shoulder into the man so violently that he flew into the air. He tumbled away but remained standing, if jarred. Skarde thrust his sword at another, and that stroke parried, he rushed in close. He took a wallop to his side, but just grunted, and punched the man square in the jaw. The man staggered, and after a further kick, sprawled on the ground. Skarde's voice boomed in triumph, but as he spun to face the rest, he saw another of his men was down.

"Fie!" Spat Skarde. "Stay up men! We will win this yet!"

Skarde cried a curse as Toran came upon him like a thunderbolt. His blows came wild, yet Skarde could not find an opening in his defense. Another of his men took a stiff blow to his neck, and then was checked roughly, throwing him to the ground. He cursed again, and there was little his last ally could do as three surrounded him and took him down with a hard kick to the back of his knees. Skarde dodged aside and dashed from Toran's assault even as his last compatriot fell. He barreled into the man who knocked him down, sending him sprawling in turn.

It was a desperate ploy. *Two more*, he thought as he tried to regain his footing after the attack, *and I might face Toran one on one*. But it was too late. One warrior clubbed him in his guts with his wooden sword, and the other grabbed him in an awkward headlock and tackled him to the ground. He landed with a thud, and had the wind knocked out of him.

Skarde forced air into his lungs with a strangled gasp and lifted himself up on his hands. Toran, smiling stood over him.

"You've lost," he said.

"Bah," Skarde said, looking Toran in the eye. "I have only lost a game."

Toran smiled at him in a way that raised Skarde's ire. "If you can't win a game, how will you win a war?"

Skarde gritted his teeth. The eyes of the men on him made his skin burn.

"A fearsome brawler you be," said Toran, "but brawling is a game for drunks and miscreants. Gul-Zagar is in need of disciplined soldiers."

Toran turned his back and began organizing the men into rows, intent on his drills, and without further distraction. Skarde stood. His limbs shook, and a fury almost overtook him. None glanced his way, and as they ordered themselves, Skarde forced himself to breathe and get a grip on his anger. *Anger. That's how Acerman got himself killed*, he thought.

His feet plodding, Skarde took a place with the others. His eyes were ready to burn a hole in anyone who so much as glanced at him, but they did not. Skarde stomped his feet as they all saluted. He pressed himself as they drilled. Not out of the humiliation he suffered, nor the desire to make amends, but because he did not want to lose again.

In the concourse above the arena floor, now unlit and shrouded in deep shadows, lurked an athletic feminine form. Sulmei, altogether naked without any adornments, spectacular or otherwise, watched the drama between Skarde and Toran in secrecy and smiled. Even if she had been discovered, few questions would have been asked. She often came to watch the men drill and was known to be fond of watching new recruits. She thrilled at the mock battle, though she knew the outcome. Toran was a worthy Mugal, skilled, determined, and thoughtful. He had met with his pick of men before, and knowing Skarde would need a lesson of this sort had drilled them beforehand. This, at least, was what she gathered from the whispers of her many lovers among the Brotherhood. Skarde's loss was foretold.

Yet her heart pumped and the hair at the back of her neck stood high as Skarde battled like a lion. She let out a cry as he toppled one opponent, and caught herself, biting her lip to silence, though in the din none caught her slip. She balled her fists, wanting to strike out at those who surrounded him as he downed a second fighter, and she wondered indulgently if he might, astonishingly, overcome Toran's trap.

"He is like a warrior of old," she whispered to herself as Skarde pulled himself out of the dust and fought to control rage and pride. "Together, we will fight. I will help him to escape captivity, and he will help me escape death." She watched the remainder of the training with roused interest.

Skarde worked hard at whatever task Toran set for them, and his bleak mood improved in dogged exertion. On the third day of ceaseless training, they marched through the high halls and out into the jungle. Skarde's eyes widened, as did his chest as they approached the gates of the citadel. He breathed deep under the sun and trees. Skarde saw he was not alone. The men about him all hastened, and their faces brightened as they left the gloom. They marched far through the paltry overgrown trails. Even in delight, Skarde thought of breaking away then and there. *But whence will I find escape? I must have a plan before I fight.*

Skarde's joy at being freed of the oppressive tunnels was diminished as they entered a vale with a familiar look. Soon they were in open fields and passed farm workers. The villagers kept their eyes down and hastened away from the marching warriors. Skarde could sense their fear and hatred, though they dared not show it openly. Worse, he recognized one or two. This was the same village that had helped him in his illness. Now he returned, among their conquerors. He kept his eyes forward and down, unwilling to look among them, though indeed none of them dared to glance at their faces.

If I can repay them for their kindness, I will, he thought, but he had no idea how that might be done.

The slopes of the volcano remained ever at his right as they marched. They drove ceaselessly along jungle paths for the most part, but also through tangling brush, and over a treacherous ash covered and rock-strewn field. They ate and drank as they kept up pace, and the sun rose and set. At long last they came to the dungeon-like mouth of the citadel, and most of the recruits' shoulders stooped as they dragged their feet along. Skarde, though he complained naught, strained as they climbed the last slope before descending into the bowels of the earth. They kept on, deep into the caverns, and it was clear they were being taken to the springs to bathe.

"Though I have marched seven or more leagues, I would that I could camp in the open air," he said to a companion at his side.

"I could sleep in this tunnel," said his companion.

Toran had led them personally from their early start. Skarde felt he must credit him for this, despite their rivalry. Afterwards, Toran led them right to the pools. He bathed with them, but left early, bidding them goodnight and promised an early start in the morning. Most lounged in the pool, groaning as their feet released the days aches into the warm water. Skarde sat on the submerged shelf of rock, and relaxed. He was exhausted, though he showed it less than most there. The men talked about their days adventure, though Skarde had little tongue for it. One of the younger recruits even had enough spirit left to stand in the midst of the pool and re-enact the adventures that had brought him to the island. Skarde laughed at his antics, but then caught bubbles surfacing behind the lad.

"Be wary, man," Skarde said. "A jet of steam will burst up from there soon."

He was so fervent in his storytelling he did not heed Skarde among all the voices.

"Move, lad, or you will be burned!"

The young man looked at Skarde, and then behind him at the churning bubbles.

"What's this?" he said.

"Your ass blows as much air as your mouth," said an older recruit, laughing at his own joke.

"Move!" warned Skarde.

"Let's see how it smells!" The younger man dipped low to sniff the bubbles, out of desire to not seem craven or just for the base humor of fighting men.

He turned his head back his crowd and laughed. Just then the geyser erupted again, and a jet of scalding water burst upward. The young man let out an ear-piercing scream, grabbed his face, and stumbled away. He collapsed in the pool a few yards away. The men straight away went silent.

"Damn fool!" Skarde said.

He rushed over to the young man's body, now limp in the water, and hauled him to the shore. They saw in the dim light that half his face was red and peeled. Skarde bent close and could hear him breathing.

"He lives at least... come, help me take him to Toran, or some other guard. There is an apothecary-priest, but I do not know how to find him," he said.

The older recruit, and two others lifted the younger, and together they took him back up the long tunnel. They came at last to their barracks, and the young man moaned in pain. His eyes rolled open, and Skarde hoped at least that he was not blinded.

"I know where to find Toran," said one.

Skarde nodded. He was one of the men he fought against a few days prior, and his suspicions of collusion were supported.

"Lay him in his bunk. I will return," said the man, running off into the dark.

Skarde watched him disappear into the murk as the others carried the young man inside. Skarde stood outside, peering along the tunnels, wondering what secrets and dangers might lurk, seen and unseen, when he heard a whisper hiss through the gloom. Away down where the recruit had run along to fetch Toran, there was a rough side tunnel, and there he could just mark the charming outline of Sulmei. She waved him hither and disappeared. He padded in her direction. At the junction of tunnels, she was nowhere to be seen. He walked further into the darkness and came across a low guttering torch as the tunnel bent off to a path to the kitchens. There, another hole had been excavated. On a hunch, he entered that near dark hole and came into a long natural tunnel. As the light faded, he saw a faint glow. Along the tunnels was a rough-hewn door frame, beyond which looked like another barracks, half made.

The walls appeared to be eked out by pickaxes and enclosed about a small space. One single sconce held a sputtering torch that lit a supple form reclining without regard for him on a long animal skin. She was unclothed, save for an uncivilized leather anklet hung with animal fangs.

"Is your compatriot hurt badly?"

"Aye, but he will heal, I think. The heat took him far worse than it did you." Skarde put an accent on that last point, hoping she might speak of her miraculous escape from harm. She remained silent and sunk deeper into the sensuous furs.

"Do I not warrant regalia of silver and jewels?" Skarde said.

"You do not strike me as a man of pageantry," Sulmei said without looking at him. "Would it please you that I sport such garish ornaments?"

"Nay," Skarde laughed. "Why put it on when I will just take it off?"

She turned and glared at him. "You are presumptuous!"

Skarde smiled. "Do you mean rude?"

"Aye, and overbold," she said.

"Is that not why you are here?"

She rolled on the skins, smiling at him. She draped her hand and curled her leg to cover herself in an idle try at modesty. He looked her over unabashed and unbuckled his belt.

"You were not touched by Gul-Zagar's words. Not as the others were." she said.

Skarde breathed deeply but continued to undress as if nothing was said. He was in dangerous territory. Though a man of the field, he knew enough at least to see that there was some courtly intrigue here.

"Leaders make speeches. Men cheer. What else can be said?" He hoped to avoid saying more.

"Was your heart not stirred?" She said, shifting her legs and making eyes at him.

"Aye," he said.

"There are more than words in his voice, and none who hear them are unmoved."

She bared herself in lewd suggestion. Skarde's heart beat hard.

"Few have the passion and a strength in them to resist, but you did, Skarde. Would you be free?"

"I would," he said.

"Then come to me, my champion…"

Chapter Eight

Toran trained the crew of recruits ceaselessly. Hardly a day went by when a man did not drop of exhaustion during bitter trudges or was injured in intense drilling. All found their way back to health soon enough and worked double to catch up. Only a handful of hearties escaped this suffering, and Skarde was chief among them. It was not for skiving off, for he threw himself into Toran's lessons when it became clear that he had much to offer. With no clear path of escape from the island, Skarde availed himself to his utmost of the circumstances. He became something of an unofficial second in command to the recruits, though Toran did not endorse the notion.

Little time did Skarde have to ponder his circumstances, but in the moments between one thing and the next, his mind often came to Sulmei. He thought too often of her smooth skin and hard muscles, her beauty, and her lusty embraces. He shook his head to clear these thoughts away. An over-fondness for drink had led to his current circumstances, his desire for an enticing woman might lead to another disaster. *Would I not find a more suitable companion in some quiet village?* He laughed at himself and found himself still thinking of that netherworld dwelling witch. When he could keep his mind away from tantalizing thoughts, he wondered again who she was and what she wanted.

'*Skarde. Would you be free?*' she asked, as if she, too, would be free. He cursed himself that he did not question her on her role in this strange place. They had made love, again and again, and before his thoughts turned to conversation, she provoked him again. Then, after hours of entwining, and without word, she slid away into the darkness. *She seems to roam free, but is she too held captive? Why? Is she in danger? My skull is not suited for these intrigues,* he thought, and he applied himself to the challenges Toran set with vigor enough to drive away vexing doubts.

Weeks passed and Skarde almost forgot his desire to escape. He learned much of swordplay, and much of the commander's art, as Toran also lectured with a pompous nose in the air. Skarde held any rebuke behind his tongue. He cared not for lofty philosophies, but Toran's instruction cleft to a practical bent. On an occasion, Toran quoted the philosopher of old, Harquan, saying: "In the heart of madness, also lies pearls." Skarde raised his eyebrows dismissively at this, but the words stuck in his thoughts. Skarde thought now of these words and others Toran said.

"In the heart of madness," Skarde whispered to himself in a moment of quiet in the bathing pool, "is surely where I am now. The pearls... the time given to me and the teachings. There is this opportunity... and what other? And what dangers?"

He saw naught of Sulmei, nor now thought much of her save when he lay down and his mind wandered to women. Tales about her were told among the other recruits – tales that turned his own ears red. He began to think that she saw him as a plaything.

One day during hard drilling in the pit, Sulmei appeared in the shadows of the benches above them and settled upon the dais at the foot of Gul-Zagar's throne. *She dares not sit on it, even when The Master is not present*, he thought.

She watched them with a casual indifference on her face. Skarde tried to catch her eye, but when she did not return the look, he shrugged and put his mind to his work. By chance, he glanced her way as he fended off a round of attacks in mock combat and caught her eyes, and in them was a glint of anger. He had little time to consider why she might have taken offense with him and was immediately forced to focus on the task at hand. When he managed another look, she seemed melancholy. Soon after that, she had disappeared.

Weeks passed, and the time came for the end of their training. Skarde, and most others reveled in their swordsmanship, the efficacy in which they worked as a unit, and their new understanding of the craft of war. Skarde again began to think of open skies, the clash of swords, and the taste of victory. Some men would join the citadel guard, the men who maintained their lair and held mastery of the island, while others would join the corsairs, and sail as pillagers of sea and port.

Skarde was confident that he would be placed as a corsair. They would be the first to despoil the loot gained by piracy, and on the forefront of whatever war Gul-Zagar was planning. He was eager to see what might unfold. And of course, sailing far and wide, he would have easy opportunity to go freelance should things not unfold to his liking.

At long last, the ceremony to mark the end of their training and to assign them their place came. They were lined up in rows in the training pit. There, Toran, Tyhomir, and a small gathering of his officers stood in armor, ceremonial splendor, and red capes. As Skarde looked about him, he could see excitement in his fellow's eyes. He bounced on his heels, almost unable to contain his energy. *Time to leave these caves*, he thought.

Tyhomir gave a speech of the kind Skarde came to expect from commanding officers, but even a long jawing could not dampen his spirits. The speech came to an end, the men cheered in unison, and Toran stepped forward.

"Come now, and receive your sword and service, O brother, and stand with your fellows," Toran said, getting right to the point.

One of the officers took a sheathed sword from an ornate carven stand and handed it to Tyhomir. Tyhomir handed it to Toran, who took it with a respectful nod.

"Remnat!" Toran said, and the man himself strode forward.

"Take this sword and be accepted among our corsairs," Toran said.

Remnat, brimming with pride, took the sword and bowed. Tyhomir motioned to the right, and Remnat stood under a ship's flag upon a tall pole.

"Jandal!" cried Toran, and the next man in the procession stood forward. "Take this sword and be accepted among our troops."

Jandal bowed and took the sword and stood under a red pennant to Tyhomir's left.

Skarde waited stock still as the recruits took their place. The crowd dwindled, and Skarde's jaw tightened. He noted his own sword was not among the collection. Most of the swords were newly forged. Perhaps he would receive one of those, but a suspicion grew in him. At last, he stood alone, facing the entire cadre.

"Skarde!" called Toran.

Skarde approached Toran, standing before him. His face was a mask, but tense. It was not Tyhomir who brought forth a sword, but another of Toran's men, bearing a cloth sack. From it, he pulled a lash and a short club. He held them forth, and Skarde took them. He looked at them, his brows knotted.

"Take the whip and the cudgel and be accepted among our mine guard," Toran said, his voice almost cracking.

A fury rose in Skarde. His jaw clenched and his fists bulged as they clamped hard about the hafts. To beat Toran with these slaver's tools would be a just revenge. *But I would not kill the bastard with these, and I would fain to kill him.* Mastering his rage, Skarde looked at Toran, who more than guessed his thoughts. Toran mouth contorted in a cruel grin, and he all but laughed after enjoying a moment of Skarde's pain. He turned and left in procession with Tyhomir, leaving the lower officers to direct them further at the ceremony's end.

None of the men spoke to Skarde or looked him in the eye as they broke and set off toward their new berths. His anger was plain, but they had their own successes to celebrate. The corsairs cheered as they were led topside. The troop were led to new quarters. Skarde was led by a single officer along with the troops 'til they split off down a tunnel that led to the bath springs.

"I've been instructed to bring you directly to your new quarters," the officer said apologetically.

He is rueful, Skarde thought. As they travelled the dark, silent passages, he mastered his fury and mused that the man was not a craven, if not a friend. He might even bow his head to the injustice of Toran's decision. *Yet that will not help my cause any more than killing him.*

Long before they reached the baths, they turned off into another side tunnel, and delved downward. They came to a grim cavern and set before them was a large iron bound set of doors.

"The mines," the officer said.

"A gaol inside a gaol," Skarde said.

"A curse on you, old man!" Skarde spat. "Bring me my sword!"

Absi scowled down at Skarde and shook his head. "Watch that sharp tongue, boy, before you cut your own throat with it."

"My possessions were to be brought to me! Now I find my sword stolen!"

"I am no thief, fool," Absi said, his nose wrinkling. "I have already explained this to you, Thick-Ears. You are a slave-guard now. Swords do not compel slaves, they kill them. Dead slaves do no work. Your trade is now with the lash."

"Pah. I am reduced to a bully!" Skarde said.

"You have not been reduced but lifted up! You serve the will of the Master, an exalted position! You've the look of a mercenary, but you are no longer an aimless freebooter. You have no personal possessions but a great destiny."

Skarde shook his head at the dusky old man. Though he wore a coat of mail, he had the look of a money counter and the tongue of a priest. Skarde gritted his teeth and fought back his urge to scale the rock face and tear apart the iron bars through which Absi looked down. Even if he could do it, killing him would get him nowhere. *There will come a chance, old man,* Skarde thought, *which may run grim for you.*

"Very well, man," Skarde said.

"Captain," Absi said. "I am your captain, not your man. I will send a brother about in the morning to show you the ways of the mines. Go to your chamber."

Skarde swallowed sour words. Gritting his teeth, he passed through an archway into the smaller tunnels that delved into the volcano. He went to the small room which the other officer had shown him, before he hastily left the mines. His cell. He lay in his cot, brooding in grim melancholy on the dark turns of fortune. Above him, he held his hand, a mere outline in the near total blackness. He gazed long at it, rueing its emptiness, and willing, if he might, a sword to appear in it.

"These Southerners believe in fate," Skarde spoke aloud to the darkness. "What use is fate if it leads me to a dark hole? I will win back my sword even if I must set the entire mountain on fire!"

Skarde lay back and slept fitfully. He prided himself on being able to sleep wherever he might, in the rough or in a busy camp. Noise might not have bothered him, but some low deep rumbling teased at the edge of his consciousness. In the black silence he heard a shuffle, a creak, and an occasional cough echoing through the tunnels. *Men*, he thought, *restless in their beds also*. But there was also a deep, dull rumbling, almost inaudible, and far, far away. His mind dwelt long on what it was, despite wishing rather for sleep.

At last, the rumbling stopped, but Skarde dreamed of some god in the depths, hammering at the roots of the earth. The hammering became a dull clack, and Skarde's door swung open. He opened an eye by a slit, and a dark figure framed in torchlight stepped forward, one soft footstep, and one harsh clack. Skarde moved not but recalled in his mind the cudgel which he kept within arm's length on his bed.

"Are you awake?" a young voice said.

"Aye," Skarde said, remaining motionless. "I rest but one ear and one eye at a time."

"Very good," the young man said as Skarde rolled on to his elbow to look him over. "I am Peg-Leg. I will show you about the mines, our ways, and what is expected of you."

"Skarde," he said, introducing himself. "Thank you for your hospitality. Sounds like the day will be wonderful. It is day, is it?"

"It is," Peg-Leg said.

"One can never be sure. Tell me, Peg-Leg, do those blessed with our duty ever get to see the sun?"

"Our duty rarely takes us outside, but it is not unheard of," he said.

"Marvelous," said Skarde rising. "Let us explore this dismal hole."

Peg-Leg waited patiently as Skarde stretched and pissed in a pot. He retrieved his cudgel, tucked it into his belt and walked out the door. Right away, Skarde heard dull tinks and chipping sounds, some far off and some near. They passed many small tunnels, chambers and drops but soon they came to a large, rugged chamber, which clamored with the sound of picks. Thirty slaves chiselled away at the walls of glistening grey and ruddy stone. Upon a dais of cut stalagmite stood a man Skarde recognized, his face stern, his nose in the air, and his hooked hands at his hips.

"Here is a rich chamber. We gather much iron here. The finest in the South," Peg-Leg said. "Once the slaves have filled their baskets, they haul them back to the hall of counting... the chamber in which Absi greeted you."

"And what is his name?" Skarde asked, pointing at the imperious guard.

"We call him No-Hands," Peg-Leg said.

Skarde laughed, and his mirth thundered off the hard walls and echoed down the tunnels. All in the chamber turned to gaze at him. The guard saw him, recognized him, and sneered in abject hate.

"Ah, my old friend!" Skarde said. "So, they call you No-Hands now? An apt name if a bit blunt."

"Erbiz is my name, whatever they call me here. And what shall we call you? Ever-Chained, perhaps?"

Skarde scoffed and thumbed the cudgel at his side.

"You are acquainted, then?" Peg-Leg said, placing himself between the two.

"Aye," No-Hands said. He held up his arms, displaying two thick hooks. "We met in the jungle."

"Now I see," Peg-Leg said. "I have heard the tales. That is in the past. We have no quarrel. We are brothers. Let us have peace."

"Aye, with luck, we might," No-Hands said flatly.

Skarde bowed. "Let us hope for the best and cross our fingers."

No-Hands glared like death at him.

"Yes. We should move on, Skarde," Peg-Leg said.

He clacked forward quickly and Skarde followed at a saunter. Many of the slaves glanced timidly at his face before turning back to their work. He thought he saw in many of their eyes a laughter withheld. *Any jab against a slaver...* Skarde thought. *And soon they will hate me also, though whatever comes I will not tyrannize them.* Peg-Leg led him on in silence. As they approached another cavern, Skarde could hear the clank of pick against stone, and a dim light. Peg-Leg halted and turned to Skarde.

"Here we will meet another brother. I hope you will be more courteous. These mines are our home... at least for now. We are the only company we keep for the most part."

"Aye," Skarde said. "No-Hands and I have a history..."

"The tale of the slaves' escape," Peg-Leg interrupted, "and your battle in the jungle is well known to us all. We are fighting men. We know it was your duty to escape an enemy."

"Aye, he and his fellows dragged me here…"

"I am his fellow, and now you are as well."

Skarde nodded. "I will be courteous to our brother."

Peg-Leg looked Skarde in the eye, apparently satisfied for the moment, and led on. The next chamber was slanted at a steep angle. Here, another twenty slaves chipped away as a gruff man with a deep, ugly scar over his right eye spoke with one after another. When he spotted them, he approached and was introduced as One-Eye. They travelled on and Peg-Leg advised Skarde of his duties. As they toured the grim tunnels, they came across other brothers: Burned-Man, a man whose flesh was ravaged by a fire, Grim-Face, whose skeleton-like visage was also touched by flame, Left-Arm, who was missing his entire right arm, and others, all of whom had one grave injury or another.

"We find all manner of gems and metals here. Iron, silver, gold, garnet, ruby… and more beside. How such a boon came to be, I do not know. You must fill quotas, set by Absi, and command your slaves as you will to meet your goal. It would be best to speak lightly with Absi."

Skarde shook his head. "Too late. Damn my sharp tongue again," he laughed.

"Perhaps by the merit of your work you can redeem yourself," Peg-Leg said.

Skarde shook his head. "I see you are in earnest, so I will not mock you. A fighter am I by profession, not a taskmaster."

"We are all warriors, doing as we must," Peg-Leg said.

"No offense, my friend," Skarde said, "But you and the other brothers down here are cast-aways. Is it not true? You have been maimed in battle, bravely no doubt, and are rewarded with a black prison."

Peg-Leg looked about, wary of listening ears. "Do not speak like that. It would seem disloyal to some."

"Is it not so?" Skarde said.

Peg-Leg's jaw clenched, and anger flashed through his eyes, or perhaps it was sadness. Brooding, he led Skarde on and continued the tour of the mines. As they circled back, Skarde looked ruefully on Peg-Leg.

"I meant no insult to you when I spoke earlier, Peg-Leg," Skarde said. "I will not speak of the matter again."

Peg-Leg said nothing for a long dark corridor, lost in thought, then he spoke. "If you, by luck and by effort, fulfill your quotas and more, you might earn your way to a new post. None here have done it. As you say we are..." Peg-Leg tapped his peg at the ground, "unsuitable for other duties. But you are uninjured."

Skarde nodded in thanks. They came, at length, to Skarde's cell.

"One last thing I must teach you," Peg-Leg said. "It is the most important, and so I left it 'til the last so it may be impressed upon you."

"Aye?" Skarde said.

Peg-Leg fished around in the pouch that hung from his belt and produced out a rough stone. He held it up and passed it to Skarde. "Look upon this, as I speak and recall it clearly."

Skarde examined it. It was a whitish mineral of six-sided rough-hewn crystal prisms jumbled together. Inside their milky surfaces ran tiny ruddy spears, and along one side of the stone, it appeared as if a black dust was pressed into it.

"I've never seen anything like this. Why is this valuable?" Skarde said.

"That is not so valuable, as I am allowed to keep it. What is valuable is the metal which is found often as squarish slivers among the crystals. It glistens like polished steel but is a dark grey. Should you find even a shaving the size of a fingernail, bring it with all haste to Absi. To find any brings reward. To not bring it right away means punishment. We have been told its worth is greater than any amount of iron or gold we might find."

Skarde stared in wonder at the stone, his mind guessing at what purposes such a metal might be put to.

"A mysterious thing this is," he said. "What is it used for?"

"I know not," Peg-Leg said. "But I guess the Master has some mystical use for it."

Skarde turned the stone in his hand and let torchlight glint from its many facets. At length, he handed it back to Peg-Leg.

"No. Keep it," said Peg-Leg. "And rest now. Tomorrow, you will have little."

Chapter Nine

Day and night were meaningless in the Tartarean depths of the mine. Day after day, Skarde oversaw his slaves and was neither kind nor cruel to them. He kept apart from them and did not wish to know them. Familiarity could only hinder him. Yet too soon, he learned their names and he cursed his heart. He considered that, since he had no plan for escape, pity could hardly hinder no goal at all. A few of them he knew from the boat that dragged him to this accursed isle. *I join them after all, a slave as much as them in all but name*, he rued.

He had little need to whip them. Verily, he had no taste for it. They seemed to know what work needed doing and did it. *Do they prefer their new, sullen master to their old? Or rather, do they just hate me less.* Skarde considered that any one of them might bash his skull in with their picks if he were not wary. He was not wary. In his melancholy, he became reckless.

Now came a thunder, dull and clanging from the depths of the earth. He sensed it as an unsettled feeling at first, nagging at his senses as a vague unease. Then, it could be heard between the tapping and ringing of the slave's work. He approached a young man who had sat near him on the slave galley and fought with him in his bid to escape.

"Do you hear that, Tarsazi? Like drums in the depths of the earth?"

"Lord, I do," he said.

"What think you of it?"

"I have heard it since I came here, months ago," he said. "Others speak of it and have heard it before me. They say spirits of the earth are angry, and will bring fire, ash, and death from the roots of the world."

"And what do you say?" Skarde asked.

"I do not know, but I like it not."

As they shared stories, he came to like Tarsazi. Skarde believed him to be a thoughtful man, but also full of piss and venom in a fight. *Spirits of the Earth?* Skarde held doubts when men spoke of spirits. *More like that answers to these mysteries are of a more earthly nature,* he thought, *though here, a sorcerer is caught up in things.* Skarde paced the dingy course of the cave his crew worked, and the dull thunderous blows seemed to grow. After a long while, he came to a decision. He strode to the end of the cavern where a rough arch served as an entrance to the tunnels and took a torch from the wall. Without any word to his men, he dove into the dark to follow the sounds.

The stone swallowed him, and he felt alone in the world. The clang of the picks on stone faded and he heard his own footsteps and breathing echoing off the hard close walls. He stood still and held his breath. He could hear it – deep clanging – and as he shut his eyes and tried to guess its direction, he could feel it in his bones. His lungs burned and he took another breath. *It seems to come from every direction*, he thought, *yet it is louder here*. At a loss, he kept moving onward, stopping here and there to ken its source. He traveled through a larger way and passed a small group of slaves lugging an enormous wheelbarrow. Behind them, No-Hands snarled at them to hasten.

"Where do you go, Ever-Chained?" He said spitefully. "Have you not duty to attend?"

"My name is Skarde," he said in a firm and calm voice, and did not stop to explain his actions.

On he went, ignoring a curse from No-Hands. He entered the main thoroughfare. It was empty, and he could catch the echoes of work from a half dozen gangs. He turned deeper into the volcano and jogged on.

"Skarde!" he heard behind him.

He thought for a moment that No-Hands had followed him. He closed a fist hard about his truncheon, thinking that his rival might need a strong argument. He turned about, grim eyed. Skarde's taut jaw melted into a smile.

"Belgeti, my friend!"

Belgeti ran over and gazed up at the giant. "What brings you here?"

"A madness of one kind or another," Skarde said.

"Oh?" said Belgeti. "I'm in."

"Either fumes from the depths have affected my senses, or I hear a drumming in the earth."

"As if from far away," Belgeti said.

"So? I am not mad?"

Belgeti shrugged. "You may be. You have that look in your eye. Yet the mad often see and hear things which are true. I have heard it also."

"Are *you* mad?"

"Yes!" Belgeti said cackling.

Skarde roared in laughter for the first time since he set foot in these caves.

"Do you know aught of its source?"

"Come," Belgeti said bidding Skarde come closer. "I will show you this first."

He held up his hand and in his palm was a pale jumble of crystals, shot through with crimson, the same that Peg-Leg had given to him. Skarde examined it closely.

"Look," Belgeti said, pointing at it.

Among the crystals was a roughly rectangular column of dark grey metal the size of two finger joints. It seemed at once rough-hewn and natural, yet polished, as if it sprung from the earth smelted.

"Grey-metal," Belgeti said.

"So, this is the thing they covet so greatly," Skarde said.

"Aye," Belgeti said. "Peg-Leg sent me to give it to Wrinkles right away. He won't mind if I show you around first."

"My thanks," Skarde said. "Let us be quick."

Belgeti led him at a loping pace deeper into the mines. They ran a long arc through the mountain and hopped down into a sloping crevasse. It led past what looked like an abandoned work site. Therein was a wall of timbers held to the wall by two thick posts and closed shut with a dozen planks.

"As I've heard, they found much wealth here, but they shut it up months ago. Some say the noise you've heard comes from past this wall."

Skarde looked over the construction. Like everything else he had found in the underground citadel, it was well built. He put his hands to the smooth wood and pulled with all his might. His muscles bulged and he gritted his teeth. With a grunt, he gave all he could. It made not so much as a creak.

"Was this made to keep us out, or keep something in?" Skarde asked.

Belgeti shrugged. That moment, they both turned their heads to the blocked passage as a deep thudding was heard. *Doom, doom, doom*, it beat. Skarde leaned forward, touching the planks with his fingertips. He placed his ear to the boards and held his breath. *Doom, doom*.

"It is coming from beyond," he said.

"Aye, and let it stay beyond," Belgeti said.

"Aren't you curious?" Skarde said.

"I am, but I am not a cat and have but one life. They say slaves delved deep and angered the spirit of the volcano. It would be best not to anger it further."

"Bah. Any more talk of spirits and you can chatter tales with old wives."

"Hmm," Belgeti said, a glint in his eye. "How old?"

Skarde laughed. "We should go."

By the same path they went back. He pondered the booming sound, the talk of spirits, and the rare metal that Belgeti showed him. They entered the main concourse, as Skarde wondered of its origin.

"Why do you think there is such an abundance of riches here?" Skarde asked Belgeti.

"Do you wonder if the spirit down below brings them?" Belgeti asked.

"It seems like a likelihood," Skarde said.

"I thought you do not believe in spirits," Belgeti said.

"Not on the whole, but when a wizard is involved…"

"Aye. Some of us say that Gul-Zagar has made a pact with the spirit to bring gifts from the very foundations of the earth. My people had shamans, but they had no such power. It would seem a mad thing to make pacts with the spirit of a volcano. They are hot tempered."

"They surely must be…" Skarde began but was interrupted by a shout.

"Ho, scoundrels!" a voice shouted.

Skarde saw that just ahead was No-Hands walking with Wrinkles. He pointed at them and spat.

"Shirking their duties, as I said, Absi," No-Hands said.

Skarde shook his head. "You frustrating imp," Skarde said as he approached. "I asked Belgeti to show me about."

The two pairs faced off with each other, and Wrinkles looked questioningly at Skarde, then to Belgeti.

"And what of you?" Wrinkles said.

"I was sent to deliver this," Belgeti said, holding up the rock.

"Ah!" Wrinkles said, stepping forward to take it. "Not a bad find," he said, looking it over.

"You are to take this to Absi right away!" No-Hands hissed. "You know you must be punished!"

Belgeti stiffened his back and stared into the distance, his face proud and grim.

"For what reason?" Skarde asked. "He brought you the damn stone!"

"You are unlettered, Ever-Chained..."

"My name is Skarde."

"You do not know the rules, so do not speak," No-Hands said.

Skarde clenched his fists.

"He is correct," Wrinkles said, striding between them before blows were exchanged. "Belgeti, you know that no delay is permitted in delivering the Grey-metal. You must face ten lashes. You shall face punishment after the work shift."

"Absi!" Skarde raised his voice. "Belgeti only did as I asked. Punish me if you must."

"I have spoken," Absi said.

No-Hands laughed. "If Ever-Chained is responsible, then make him responsible for the punishment? Let him swing the whip, Absi!"

"Very well. Let it be so," Absi said.

Skarde drew a breath in rage and would have spoken harsh words. Belgeti turned to him, caught his eye, and shook his head. Skarde clenched his jaw and turned his eyes to the ground.

"It's settled," Wrinkles said. "Begone, Ever-Chained. Back to your work. When the bell rings return to the Gate Hall for your duty.

Skarde returned to his allotted mine under a dark cloud. Hours turned as slow as whole days in the unseen sky far above. The men trudge through their labors, sensing something amiss and unwilling to delve for trouble. Like a toll for the dead, the work bell rang at last, and Skarde escorted his crew back to their quarters. In grim silence, he trod to the Gate Hall.

There, the bullies assembled beside Absi in the center of the hall. Skarde kept his head high, though he looked no one in the eye. He stood apart, close to the whipping post, set into the stone at the edge of the cave, opposite Absi's barred office. Another bully arrived, and another after that, and at last Peg-Leg arrived, clacking loudly on the hard floor. Belgeti followed close behind, his face a mask.

"Wrinkles!" Peg-Leg demanded. "He's my man, and I want to know what this is all about."

"Don't raise your voice to me, Peg-Leg. Come," Absi said, waving him close.

Wrinkles spoke in a low voice to Peg-Leg. Nearby, No-Hands grinned like a gleeful devil. Wrinkles handed Peg-Leg a length of rope. Peg-Leg glanced darkly at Skarde, and turned back to Wrinkles, nodding. Peg-Leg returned to Belgeti, who stood like a stone statue, and waved him forward. Without a word from either, Belgeti walked to the whipping post and made no struggle as Peg-Leg bound him to it by his wrists.

"Well," Wrinkles said. "Do your duty!"

Seeing no benefit in delay or words, Skarde paced behind Belgeti a whip length, and plucked it from his belt. *Forgive me*, Skarde thought, but did not say. He could not ask it of Belgeti yet.

He swung back his arm and lashed out. The whip struck Belgeti's back. He flinched yet stood silent and still.

"What is that!" No-Hands cried. "You wield the whip like a lover's lash at a whore house. Put that arm to use!"

"Agreed," Wrinkles said. "That lash does not count toward the tally. Do your duty properly."

Skarde stared at the pair, teeth clenched. He turned back to Belgeti, determined not to extend his torture any longer than needed.

"Nine Hells!" Skarde swore.

He lashed out again and the whip cracked against Belgeti's back, drawing blood.

"One," Wrinkles called out as if he were counting barrels of ore.

Skarde struck again and again, and Belgeti stood stock still and silent at every lash. *Were only you as silent, Wrinkles*, Skarde thought as the taskmaster counted. Belgeti's back dripped blood, dappling the ground red as Skarde swung his last blow. The whip cracked and stung the bound man, and at last he let out a sound, low and guttural.

"That is his ten," Peg-Leg said.

Without waiting for an order, he strode over to the post and untied Belgeti's hands. The injured man swayed but stood. His eyes were clamped shut, and his mouth pursed as Peg-Leg led him away at a gentle pace.

Skarde had little to say to anyone for days. His black mood affected his crew, who worked listlessly. It came then as a jolt when the men suddenly cheered. Skarde's eyes bolted open, and he looked upon the celebrating men, their shadows flickering in the ruddy torchlights.

"Ho, what now?" Skarde said, his voice like hard scrabble.

The men approached and Jarrod, an older, hard worn slave, approached, holding forth a mineral.

"The Grey, boss," Jarrod said. "A good chunk too. Maybe we'll get some time off."

Skarde took the rock and examined it. "Good find," he said flatly. "Twice the size of the other I've seen."

He handed the rock back to Jarrod, who dropped it in a pouch. "Come, man, you will give this to Wrinkles, and I will accompany you. Take a moment of rest, lads," he said to the crew.

They cheered as they left, glad for a few moments of rest. Jarrod rushed to the entrance to the tunnels and grabbed a torch but did not drop his pick. Skarde, too, snatched up a torch, wary of being reliant on another for light in the tunnels. They sped to the Gate Hall. There, Wrinkles smiled down through the bars that guarded his post. He reached down and took the stone from the smiling Jarrod.

"A good one, aye," Wrinkles said.

"Yes," Jarrod said.

"Well," Wrinkles said, looking at Skarde, "this almost makes up your poor yields. Still... take two hours off, yourself and your men, and I'll make sure there's some meat in your supper tonight."

"Thank you, lord!" Jarrod said.

Skarde nodded. They left, and as they did, some flame sparked in Skarde's darkened soul. Hate, macabre glee, or some other madness, he cared not to make an attempt to name it.

"Ah, meat," Jarrod said. "I haven't had a bit of meat between my teeth in a long while. Something to look forward too!"

"Aye," Skarde said wryly, his breath coming quicker. "Good times ahead!"

"The lads will be happy when they hear. They haven't had much to smile about for a long while." Jarrod said.

Skarde slapped Jarrod on the back. "You tell them, good man!" He said. "Give me the pick."

"What? Yes, lord," he said, handing the pick to Skarde.

Skarde swung the tool over his shoulder and strode along the main concourse of the mine. He turned to Jarrod. "My name is Skarde, Jarrod, not lord. Don't forget to tell the boys to take a few hours for rest!"

"Aye, Skarde," he said, and he ran off toward their cavern.

Skarde set off at a quick pace, and his long legs carried him swiftly. *Meat and a brief respite!* Skarde turned over the reward in his mind, laughing to himself and wishing he could get his hands around Absi's throat. He had pondered Peg-Leg's suggestion that he might earn further freedom in the Stygian blackness of his cell at night... he did not know where the sun shone in the land of the living. Far off, he could hear the echoing cheers of his crew. *They are as glad as Jarrod was to be tossed a bone like a dog.* He stood in the cavern with the sloping crevasse that led to the forbidden tunnel.

"I can not blame them. I, too, shall be a dog soon if I don't escape or at least try," he said to the flickering shadows a stalagmite threw against a wall from the light of his torch in a vaguely manlike shape.

He laughed at his growing madness, and as his black mirth quieted, he heard it. *Doom. Doom.* He smiled. *Luck is with me... make good use of it!* He thought as he climbed downward.

Presently, he was before the plank shuttered tunnel. He pressed his ear to the wood. For a moment he thought he heard a faint footstep, but then clear as ever he heard the pounding deep beyond. *Doom. Doom. Doom.*

He threw the torch upon the ground and swung the pick about as if he were eager for a fight. "I don't know what I seek... but I can not rest here."

He swung the pick, and it lodged squarely between rock and plank. He stood on the far side of the blocked mouth, grabbed the handle, and pulled with all his might. The board creaked and some dust scattered to the ground.

"Hells," he said. "Has the wizard himself fixed these damned nails into the rock?"

He pulled again, rocking his body violently on the pick handle. "Thunir's Axe! I will... open you!"

His thick muscles strained against the boards. At last, something crunched, and more dust scattered. The bolt had been loosened by an inch. Now Skarde worked to open it further, which took a few moments, but did not require a titanic effort. He cursed when he discovered one board did not suffice for his bulk to pass, and with straining thews and curses, he loosened a second.

For a moment, he stood and rested, happy that he had opened a new road for himself, though he knew not where it led. *If it leads anywhere. But even nowhere is not here, and so an improvement.* He tossed the pick, and the torch through, bent low and looked. It seemed like an unremarkable passage. He shrugged and squeezed through the opening. He picked up the pick and the torch and stepped carefully forward. Ahead there was a turn, and he strained to see about the corner. *Doom, Doom,* came the thunder in the earth, much clearer than ever, though still muffled.

So eager was he to discover its secret that as he rounded the corner, he failed to notice a black shape slink silently between the planks he had pried open.

He moved on, and a short way ahead, he came to a chamber. There, stalagmites and stalactites decorated the floor and roof, as in much of the mines. The walls looked hacked and chipped, and he guessed that it was mined at some point in the past. At the left side of the cavern, a large hole with sharp edges appeared in the floor. He stepped lightly forward and peered over the lip. After a drop of fifteen feet or so, there was a floor littered with scree. His eyes opened in surprise. Under him lay a corpse whose blackened drooping flesh might have been some months dead. There were no rock walls under the lip of stone where he stood. His eyes traced the curved walls of the chamber beneath him. It seemed as if he stood on the edge of a bubble. He tapped the ground at the lip of the hole, and it crumbled, falling into the hollow below.

"Funir's wing," he muttered, wondering at his luck that he had not broken the thin floor on which he no doubt stood.

He moved to withdraw, but out of nowhere, a dark shape flew at him from behind and struck a mighty blow to his back. Skarde grunted and stumbled into nothing. Darkness swallowed him up and the onrushing ground slammed the wind out of him. He lay still for a moment, pain shooting through his every fiber. He pressed against the ground, his limbs throbbing, numb and aching, and he rose on all fours. *Nothing broken.* He tried to inhale, but nothing would come. His lungs felt flattened, his chest burned in agony. The world spun as he struggled for air, screaming at death. With agonizing effort, he drew breath. Air trickled into his lungs with a croak, and he could only gasp for a tortured minute.

"Ever-Chained," called a voice above him.

Skarde looked about. He was in the rounded chamber with neither his pick nor his torch. The faint ruddy light illuminated the corpse only five feet from where he knelt now.

"Ever-Chained," the voice called again. "You live."

Get a rope, Skarde tried to say, but his voice was only a hiss. He struggled to turn and stand up on his knees, straining to see the figure above him.

It was No-Hands.

He held a torch, his hook serving almost as well as fingers, and looked down upon Skarde, gloating.

"Hells," Skarde said.

"It would have been easier for you if the fall broke your neck like it did for that slave beside you," he said.

Skarde looked at the body. *No-Hands will leave me here! He's had his revenge.* He looked back up. "Do you expect me to beg for mercy?"

"I had hoped for it," No-Hands said. "But if you deny me the pleasure, I will still rest easy tonight, knowing you sleep with the dead, and are soon to join them."

Why bother to hold my sharp tongue now, I wonder? "Aye for the best," Skarde said. "I did not expect you to give me a hand."

No-Hand's smirking face snapped into a mask of hate. He kicked at Skarde's fallen pick, and it tumbled into the hole over his head. Even battered and winded, Skarde moved as fast as a mongoose. The handle battered his back, but the heavy iron clattered harmlessly beside him.

"Fool!" No-Hands spat. "Your clever mouth has won you a nameless grave. When The Master's work here comes to an end, we shall go on to fight for a glory of which you could not dream! I will see the Sun again, and rule with the Iron Brotherhood all beneath it!"

Skarde laughed. No-Hands stared at him, incredulous that Skarde now looked at him with a gloating expression.

"Have you lost your mind?" No-Hands said.

"Madness is a subject that oft seems to arise down here. I have not lost my mind, but you certainly have," Skarde said.

"Your taunts are meaningless."

"Oh? The Master is a man of war, I think, with a cold nature. He has found a use for you in this pit. When he no longer needs this wretched hole, your use is ended. You will be tossed away. You are no longer a fighting man."

"I have earned glory!" he said.

"Good man! Spend it well in whatever heap you land in."

No-Hands face twisted into a rage, his eyes looking for something else to cast down at him. Finding nothing at hand, he settled on words.

"Die slowly, Ever-Chained!"

Chapter Ten

Skarde's hands and legs still stung with pain. No-Hands had left, along with every shred of light. Skarde stood and took a moment to recover his breath before searching the walls of the hole. There were no sharp corners. The sides sloped up gradually. Skarde felt about for a long while, seeking out with his fingertips for any juts or cracks. He had found a few, but as he climbed, the cave bent over him, making holds impossible.

Clang, Doom!

The sounds he sought reverberated from the room. Whatever it was that he sought, it was close by. Skarde dropped to his feet on the sloping surface and pointed his arm toward where he thought the sound might have come from.

"I will not die down here, by Thunir!" he swore.

He noticed that he could see his outstretched arm, only just. He could see his meandering hand as a blot of pure blackness on a background of slightly lesser blackness.

"Light? I'll be damned – there must be a source."

He crossed the dark chamber, each footstep seeking a hold before the next was taken. He placed his hands on the walls, and he raised his eyebrows. *This wall seems warmer*, he thought. He groped inch by inch along the surface, straining his eyes for any hint. Then, to his liking, he could make out his hand against the wall. He looked all about, and thought he saw a misty patch in the corner of his eye. Twisting his head beneath it he caught sight of a hole. Beyond it was the faintest dull ruddy patch of light. He put his hand in and pulled. He grunted as his muscles bulged, and a slice of rock broke away. Smiling, he tossed the little chunk into the hole. He heard it *thunk* and skitter away into a space beyond.

"Funir's Wing! I have found something!" he said.

He retreated into the chamber and felt about on the floor for the pick. His hand first came across the skull of the corpse. He spat in disgust, thankful at least that the remains were no longer wet. Moments later, he laid hands on the cool metal head of the pick.

"At last, my sharp tongue has done some good," he said, grateful to have the tool.

He returned to the wall with the faint hole of light. He took a moment to position himself. *Clang! Doom! Clang!* Came the thunder of the earth. Skarde swung at the wall, and the rock crunched under his blow. He smiled, a feeling of triumph filling his heart. *Clang! Doom! Clang!* He swung the pick in time with the rumbling sound. The stone shattered and sparks sprayed his shins. Chip after chip fell away and the ruddy light lit his legs. He swung a mighty blow and a mass as big and as thin as a shield fell away. Skarde bent low and stuck his head through the opening. He saw another chamber like the one he was in, a bubble of rock, save that a thick crack, large enough for a man to fit in ran along the far side. The leftward portion of the crack glowed red, as if a fire burned beyond.

Clang! Doom! Clang! The Earth's thunder was now loud enough to grate the ear. Skarde's heart pumped. *What lies ahead? If I must crack my way through the Nine Hells and back, I'll do so!* He dropped the pick into the newly discovered chamber. Following it, he slid several feet but landed upright. He grabbed the pick and writhed through the crack at the far end. *Doom! Clang! Doom!* The blast shook the stone beneath him. Skarde gritted his teeth at the deafening blast, and hot air brushed his cheeks. He crawled thirty feet or so, and a fiery light illuminated a craggy fence of rock ahead. The heat became almost unbearable as he pulled himself out of the crack. He lay on a ledge behind a row of stalagmite teeth.

Beyond that was a vast rounded chamber, glowing with red light and shimmering with heat. A tingle down his savage spine warned him of something uncanny, something awry. He gasped as a vast hammer rose into view above the rock fence behind which he hid. A huge hand, black as obsidian, held it and it fell with the might of a lightning stroke. *Clang! Doom! Clang!* Skarde covered his ears at the blast. Wary as a hunting cat, he lifted his eyes above the barrier. His heart chilled in terror, and he dropped low.

A giant! His face was a wide mask, stunned and incredulous at the sight.

The giant's hammer fell again, and Skarde covered his ears. He sat low for a long while, sweating in the heat and gathering his thoughts. He knew he had to take stock of the situation he had gotten himself into, but caution was needed. *There is no way to fight such a monster with this toothpick*, he thought. At length he peered over the top and his eyes swept the scene.

The cavern was a huge cauldron, half filled with burning red-hot lava. Great stalactites were draped from the ceiling, and down one poured a stream of brilliant yellow molten rock. A path of black stones jutted up from the lava and ran down the center of the chamber, like rocks providing a crossing over a stream. Near the center stood a cyclopean iron anvil, the size of a horse cart. A figure like a human woman stood nearby, between the anvil and the molten falls. Her body undulated, and glowed red like she herself were made of hot metal. As she moved and swayed the molten rock under the falls and the nearby pool glowed orange, then bright yellow as if it was heating. She plunged her arm into the burning stone and drew from it a brand of burning blue-white. Skarde shielded his eyes, it was so bright.

The giant, perhaps four times his height, took the blazing brand with a pair of tongs and set it to the anvil. His hair and beard hung down like red-copper straw, and he was arrayed in a skirt of brass mail. With a swing of his inhumanly large arms, he brought the hammer down on to the incandescent rod. Thunder rocked the air, and sparks like a spray of stars arced almost to Skarde's hiding spot. More than the tremendous noise, the blinding light of the brand, the mysterious molten woman and the gargantuan monster was an eldritch sense of sorcery. It made him dizzy, and the uncanny cavern seemed to shift in dimension. He sat back down, guarded by the rock fence.

"Hodan's beard, what have I stumbled upon!"

Skarde lay in wait for what seemed a ceaselessly long night. The hammer clanged and rumbled the stone beneath him, the blazing brand sent hard white flashes as bright as the Sun, and stark black shadows dancing about him. Skarde put the cacophony out of his mind and awaited a reprieve before he would make a further move. A crashing voice shocked him from his repose.

"Almost forged is the sixth blade," came a voice like an army of men shouting, deep beyond bass, and stony. "One more night and it shall be complete!"

"Why not finish now?" said another voice. A woman's voice, though Skarde could just hear her over the distant echoes of the giant. "Do you tire?"

"Do not jest with me, mortal! You know I tire not!" The giant boomed. "I await only the preparations of Gul-Zagar, and what sacrifice he will provide for the living blade."

"You have no play in you, Mor," the woman's voice said coquettish. "Do you speak thusly to giant women?"

"You are not a giantess," he said.

"And you are no pleasure," she said.

No more was said, and Skarde dared to peek over the wall again. Mor, the giant, inspected a long sword about as long as his forearm. The woman walked away, now too far to be seen clearly. Her flesh, no longer glowing and mortal seeming, was covered in ash. She wore no clothes, and her bare feet tread along a thin causeway of stone mere inches from flaming molten slag, indifferent to the heat. Soon after the giant took the sword and his hammer, and followed the same path as the woman, his massive bare feet shaking the volcanic stone.

Skarde sank below the fence of stalagmites and held still for long minutes. Over the thick trickling sound of the lava falls, the noise of the giant faded. Sweat trickled from his brow. His clothes were soaked with sweat, and he might have swooned had he the constitution of a lesser man. *I must move now*, he thought, *or I will slowly broil*. He looked cautiously over the fence again. The great lava chamber was empty. Directly below, there were black rocks jutting from the burning red death inches below. He examined the craggy rock wall beneath him. Below and halfway to the causeway was a rough ledge a few inches wide that might serve as a path. He grabbed his pick and surmounted the wall. As soon as he was beyond the safety of the ledge behind the fence, he felt the heat blast him like a furnace. He grabbed a bulbous outcropping of stone and gritted his teeth. It was as if he had gripped an iron frying pan that had been left over a fire too long.

"Ach!" he grimaced in discomfort.

He swung the pick, and it lodged over another stone. Hanging from the pick handle, his boots tucking on to whatever hold his feet could find; he looked down and deadly lava boiled beneath him, its terrible heat seeming to drag him toward an ashen grave. He took another painful handhold, swung his pick again, and moved as fast as he could. As he climbed down to the thin ramp, the heat grew. He gripped another hold and swore in pain. The pick slipped as he grabbed desperately with his right hand, lest he fall. The tool clunked off stone and crackled as it sank into the lava. He gasped in pain again, and he leapt for the thin ledge along the wall. Landing on the burning stone his feet, even booted, stung with heat.

"Thunir!" he swore, and he ran along the deadly course.

There was no room to balance, and he tipped to his right. He sprinted frantically, and sprang before he fell in, his thews straining. Over ten feet of molten rock he flew, only just landing upon the concourse. He dared a quick look back at the pick, sinking into the molten quagmire. Already the iron head, half sunk, glowed red, and the wooden handle blazed like a torch. His feet would soon also begin to smoke, and he ran through the great arch of stone that the woman and the giant had passed earlier. He was heedless of danger till, some fifty feet in, the heat was tolerable.

There was nowhere to hide, so he pressed himself against the wall and took a moment to rest. Sweat poured from his brow and his heart pounded. *The Nine Hells are harder to crack than I thought. One is enough.* Forcing himself to move, he rounded a corner and entered a huge corridor. Ahead was a strange blueish glow, and Skarde crept forward stealthily. The corridor opened into another huge chamber, and there upon a massive slab lay Mor, the giant.

Skarde caught his breath and ducked back out of view. *Funir's Wing! The bastard is huge!* As he lay hidden behind the rock wall, the giant was enough of a menace, but now, with nothing between them but two of the giant's strides, the monster's threat was horrific. Skarde chanced one more furtive look.

The giant lay motionless, his breath coming like the long slow strokes of bellows. He seemed to be asleep. *Asleep, and mortal*, thought Skarde, *unless the immortals themselves also must slumber*. Everything else, however, did seem beyond mortal bounds. Mor's frame was wide, like the Dwarf folk of legend, with thick bands of muscle girthier than the wrestlers of Casikiyso. Several of the magical globes lit his body, which glistened black like obsidian glass. Skarde wondered if his flesh was equally hard. Beside him was set his blacksmith's hammer, almost as large as Skarde's torso, and the giant's own sword. It was a colossal length of steel, broad, and at least twice as long as Skarde was tall. Set upon a rack near to his stone bed hung the sword he had been forging. Skarde sensed it was a mighty blade, but in its place, it looked like a dagger.

Skarde feared little to fight man or beast, but he felt dread and revulsion as he padded away from the giant's den. Leaving the corridor, he turned right again and follow the last path on this side of the lava chamber. On it went, a great stalactite dotted dome for some few hundred feet. He swore silently under his breath as at last came into view a pair of gigantic doors, now dimly lit from reflected light. As he approached the gates closely, he saw they were barred with a massive log.

"By Luwydi," Skarde swore.

The bar was a squared tree trunk, set twice his height off the ground. Even if he could have reached it, he would have struggled even to budge it from its iron brackets. Cursing, he inspected the corners for some hidden passage. None could he find. Having little choice, he resolved to return to the lava chamber.

He raced but slowed to a cautious gait as he neared the giant's lair. Soon, he stood at the entrance to the vast cavity and inspected its walls for any sign of a way of escape. At the far end the walls seemed to slope away. There might be a tunnel on the other side, but in the eerie light it was difficult to tell its shape. *I must make haste,* he thought. *The heat here is terrible. Inside that oven, death will come quickly.*

"Thunir, give me strength!" he said.

He bolted ahead. Right away his feet burned on the blistering hot causeway. As he neared the molten falls, the heat of the air seared his skin. He struggled to breathe. Sputtering embers splashed up from the pool as it swallowed the pouring liquid stone beside the gargantuan anvil. He dodged to avoid a deadly spray and ran on. The meager path thinned, and Skarde had to jump over flows of lava that crossed his path. The track appeared passable but turned a corner into another chamber. He could not see where it went.

Do I even have the strength to turn back? Nothing but death, slow or quick, awaits me there. Onward, I must! All these thoughts crowded his head in the span of a desperate heartbeat. He plunged into the unknown. The path did continue. It made a sharp turn to the right and hugged the wall, and some twenty paces ahead the lava cooled in color to a black shore on a deadly lake. His every fiber screamed in pain. He dashed over a rounded pitch-black floe and kept on 'til the air was breathable. His seared lungs gasped for succor, and he doubled over. Looking down, he saw that his boots smoked.

"Ahhhh!" He cursed in pain and fell to the ground, kicking them off his feet.

The stone beneath him was warm, but not uncomfortable. He gripped his ankles and inspected his feet. They were red, and sensitive to touch, but not yet burned. Drenched in sweat, and fighting dizziness, he took a moment to recover.

"I can't die," he spoke to the roof of the cavern. "Not yet. I will kill No-Hands first."

He rolled up and put his boots on. They, at least, were no longer on fire. He stood and groaned at the numberless aches in his body. Looking about, he saw the large passage continued some ways, and a smaller way led off to his right. With a shrug, he followed the narrower path. He trod slowly, at first in discomfort, as it climbed upwards. It opened into a large arrowhead shaped chamber decorated with rock formations. This pinched off, and Skarde slid through an opening. He saw a glow ahead and soon pushed himself out into the very same chamber before the fenced ledge over the lava chamber. He sat and laughed at himself.

"I could have saved quite a bit of trouble for myself, although... it would have been a shame to miss the giant's lair." He whispered to himself.

He crawled back into the crack from which he had come. "Mad, mad, mad. Going mad."

Back near the shore of the lava pool, he took the large tunnel and hoped for the best. As it turned, again rightward, he saw a dark patch in the floor ahead. He stepped carefully over and looked into a black hole. He reached down and grabbed the ledge, and a large flake of stone crumbled into his grasp and smaller pieces fell inward. *Another round chamber, hidden in the stone*, he thought. He guessed it was thirty feet deep. He backed up and stuck close to the walls, not wanting to break through.

He kept on, and the light from the lava pool faded until he was almost in total darkness. His eyes adjusted slowly to the gloom, and a little way on he saw a tunnel leading steeply up. He smiled, having at least some option, and took that way. He crawled up. His knees ached, his hands throbbed, and he found himself in total darkness again. He wondered how far he should go before giving up. His heart pounded, and he was exhausted like few times in his life. *Only that awful jungle water has made me feel worse*, he thought. Then he saw a faint glow. Crawling but a little further ahead he almost toppled through a hole beneath him.

Looking down, he found he was in the roof of some high chamber. The flickering light below looked to him like a lone torch set somewhere out of sight. This gave him hope, and as he scanned the ground beneath him, he saw a pick. Eyes widening, he looked for a way down. This was someone's mining chamber. It was a thirty-foot drop perhaps, and he certainly would not try such a drop on to hard stone. Leaning in, he saw there was a stalactite near the lip of the hole right under him. *I'm not going back,* he thought, and with that, he turned and clambered through the hole.

Though his hands stung, he gripped the rock tightly. Lowering himself, he wrapped his arms about the gnarled rock of the spike. He grunted as he slipped, and he held on desperately. He stopped his descent, but the stalactite became uncomfortably thin. Looking down, he saw he was over half-way to the ground.

A little further, he thought, his hands aching. He lowered himself another few feet and was almost ready to let go and bear the pain of the fall when the stone snapped. The dim chamber spun about him, and the ground struck him like a blow from the giant, and blackness took him.

Chapter Eleven

Hands grappled Skarde roughly. He recalled lying on a cold hard bed, and flickering torches. Darkness and pain. He was dreaming... fevered. *A dream*, he thought. Did he say it aloud? *A mad dream.*

"He's too damn heavy," said a voice, grunting.

"Aye, he's a big one," said another voice.

"Let's leave him here," said another.

"Grim-Face would tan our hides," said the first.

"Aye," laughed a fourth voice. "We'll take him all the way."

"He's not all bad," said the second. "No-Hands hates him, so I can't help but like him."

Skarde could not answer, and the world tumbled about him 'til he felt his familiar bed beneath him. Darkness took him again. He felt hands pressing him upright, and water filled his mouth and tickled his throat. He coughed and sputtered lest he choke.

"Drink," said a familiar voice.

Skarde coughed again and felt a water skin at his lips. He drank and the water soothed his aching throat. It was nectar as to one who has not quenched his thirst for a week. He gulped it down and gasped in relief. He took deep breaths.

"What in *Tomog* happened to you?"

"Fire. Monsters," Skarde said, his throat sore.

He looked at his hands and saw they were bandaged. He raised his head and straightened his back, and saw he was in his cell. Belgeti sat beside him.

"Your hands are blistered," Belgeti said. "Otherwise, I would think you were caught in a dream."

"Aye. A strange dream, forsooth." He curled his fingers gently and winced in silence.

"You are not badly injured. You will be fine in a few days," Belgeti said. "You have the look of a man left to roast in a desert, dry and hoarse. You are well bruised and battered to boot."

Belgeti slapped his leg and Skarde grunted in pain.

"Yet you live," Belgeti said. "So whatever adventure you've been on is a success."

Skarde laughed. "I dispute that, Belgeti. Why do you tend to me?"

"Peg-Leg told me to do so. You were found in Grim-Face's area. He had his lads move you and when Peg-Leg found out, well, here we are." he said.

"But why you? Would you rather not kill me? A fair revenge for the whipping I inflicted on you."

Belgeti sighed. "I will not say I loved you as you beat me. I have fought many men and suffered injury in battle. Then as fortunes shifted, I fought beside those very same men. As enemy, and as friend, there was respect. You dished out pain with the whip, but Wrinkles and No-Hands dished out humiliation. So, Skarde, I would kill them before I would kill you."

Skarde nodded.

"Besides, if I killed you, they would simply send someone down here even bigger and uglier."

Skarde laughed, and his throat stung. He took a long sip of water and tried to sit. His feet were red also but hurt less than his hands. Belgeti's eyes raised in concern, and he looked as if he would say something, but decided against it.

"There is a giant in the heart of the mountain, Belgeti. Four or five men in height and terrible to behold! He has a forge and hammer of titanic size."

"A giant? Do your eyes deceive you? No slight upon you, but men as hardy as you have told stranger tales after heat and thirst assailed them."

"No, I saw it aright. A giant in a cavern of lava, and a woman. Neither paid any mind to the heat," said Skarde.

Belgeti leaned in, and Skarde told his tale in full. He did not hide his desire for escape, nor his accusations against No-Hands. Belgeti listened closely. Skarde stopped in the middle of his tale. He was reminded of the fireside tales fighting men told to each other, each taller than the last, and he smiled. At last, he finished, and waited for Belgeti's judgement.

"It seems more like a fable told to children. Yet it explains the thunder deep in the earth."

"Aye, the sound was deafening beside his forge."

"Perhaps also it explains the Grey-Metal," Belgeti said.

"How so?" said Skarde.

"What color was the sword you say you saw upon the giant's rack?"

Skarde recalled the sword to his minds eye and looked upon it. "It was not like steel, it was dull, smooth… and grey!"

Skarde looked upon Belgeti, his eyes wide, and Belgeti laughed.

"You came through your trial not empty-handed, Skarde," he said. "At least we know two of The Master's secrets!"

Skarde fell back into bed. "Aye, but of what use? We are still here. I fought on the beach, I fought in the jungle, and I fought in Gul-Zagar's pit. Yet here I am. It turns out I am a slave after all!"

"Huhf," Belgeti said. "At least you need not swing a pick,"

"Aye, true. But with pick or whip, I mean to escape this prison."

Belgeti sat still and pondered his words. "Should you discover some path out of here other than death, I will fight with you."

"Good!" Skarde said.

"And I know many slaves that would also fight. Some of the bullies may join you as well."

"Aye, but death is most likely. A revolt of slaves against well trained and well armed soldiers will bring death to us all, most like," Skarde said, though his hand itched to pick up a sword.

"All paths bring death, friend. But if there is any chance of success? I would rather fight and die, than rot in here." Belgeti raised his hand and offered it. "Do not you straw-haired northmen clasp their hands when alliances are struck?"

Skarde pushed aside Belgeti's hand with his forearm and swung his feet to the ground. With gritted teeth he stood, his body aching. Belgeti stood with him, looking square up at the huge man.

"Preferably when standing," Skarde said, extending his arm.

Belgeti smiled and they clasped each other's hands. Skarde felt the pain of his blistered flesh but gripped all the harder for it.

"Will you rest?" Belgeti said.

"Nay," Skarde said. "It will beg questions should I not attend my duties, and I would not show weakness to my enemies. It would only encourage them."

Skarde sat, and pulled on his boot, slow and gentle. Readied enough for his workday, he stood and Belgeti followed him.

"I would not hold you from your duties, Belgeti," Skarde said limping on aching legs and sore feet.

"I will go with you first," he said. "Your company is a little better than hacking at rocks."

"And your praise is much like being hacked," Skarde said.

Soon, the work bell rang, and the two strolled to the main concourse. It was busy with men coming and going as the sun rose in the world far above them. Suddenly, No-Hands appeared with one of his men, and stared at Skarde with eyes wide as bowls. Skarde forced himself to move sprightly, as if he had suffered no injury.

"Good morning, No-Hands. You look as if you've seen a ghost," he said.

"Are you well?" Another bully, Black-Toad, said to No-Hands.

"Yes, of course!" he said annoyed.

Skarde held back a laugh, not half because of his aching ribs, and the pair made their way towards Skarde's area. As the caves branched off, Skarde insisted Belgeti leave him then; he would return to his men without assistance. He thanked him and Belgeti slapped his arm roughly. On Skarde went. His aching legs felt better for the walk, but his feet protested.

"Where've you been, boss?" asked Tarsazi.

The slaves were already on site, for which he was thankful. "Just poking about. You assembled here faster than I!"

"Have you been to the arena?" Tarsazi said, looking him over.

"Aye," he laughed. "In a manner of speaking. I have a task for you, Tarsazi, as my task is not quite done."

"Aye?" he said.

"Watch over the men and keep a good dig up. I shall be away for an hour or two. I'll do my best to get you and the lads some extra victuals tonight."

"Aye!" Tarsazi said.

He took a torch. Then, almost as Skarde arrived, he stepped back out of the cavern.

"Odd thing," Skarde's sharp ears heard one of the men say to Tarsazi as he left. "Grim as a hungry wolf he's been the whole time. He disappears and looks like he's fought half an army and pleased as a cat with a drumstick."

"Aye," Tarsazi said. "Gets me thinking, and thinking is dangerous."

Skarde laughed and went on lighter in step. *The bullies and the slaves are no doubt at work now*, he thought, but he moved with stealth at each intersection regardless. He came to the main concourse and listened carefully. Clear of men, he swiftly traversed it. Through abandoned tunnels he went and came at last to the shuttered tunnel.

The planks were back in place. He had come to set them back, to avoid suspicions, but the job was done for him. *No-Hands most likely*, he thought. *No doubt he hoped my body would never be found*. He tested the planks he had dislodged. The nails that held them were loose, and he felt them move with but a firm tug. He pushed them back into place. *Might No-Hands have set a watch for me? Might he be creeping down one of the tunnels right now with a gang of villains to do me murder? Nay, I surprised him this morning.* Still, he held his breath and listened. Nothing. *He will come for me soon, if not now. He hates me, the cause of his maiming and his banishment into this Tartarean hole more than he loves life in the darkness. Tonight maybe, he will come for my death.*

Skarde resumed breathing and set off. He had hardly taken a dozen steps, when he heard the unnerving rumble of the giant's hammer in his ears as much as he felt it in his feet. *Doom. Doom.* In his mind, he heard the giant's cyclopean voice. "*What sacrifice he will provide for the living blade?*" A supernatural fear ran up Skarde's spine, and he ran, despite the pain.

Skarde returned to his work with even greater caution, his mind on the skulduggery he had found himself in. His smile remained, though it seemed to the men the smile of a man determined to meet a challenge. He pondered a plan for the night when he guessed No-Hands would be done with him. At last, the work bells signaled the end of labor for the day. He accompanied his men to the mess and bandied with the mess officer.

"I won't argue," Skarde said. "The lads put in a worthy effort today. Extra rations for them, and meat if you have it."

"I can't do that, Ever-Chained, or Absi will ring my ears," he said.

"I am Skarde. And I'll ring your ears first, man. You can tell Wrinkles what you like."

"Fine," he said. "It's not worth the fight, for you or for me."

"You're a good one. My thanks!" Skarde said.

He oversaw the doling-out of food and then set upon devouring his portion. He left without a word and returned to his work site, now limping but steady. He retrieved a pick, and returned to his cell, careful that no one saw him or his misappropriated tool. Laying on his bed, he shut his eyes, leaving a candle to burn beside him. He napped; one eye open for a few hours. *Enough sleep for a campaigner*, he thought.

It was deep night when he arose, the candle beside him growing dim. He bundled straw together in something resembling a human form and shaped his blanket about it.

"It wouldn't fool a blind dog," he whispered. "But it will have to serve for but a momentary distraction."

He hid his pick beside his personal trunk and lay down behind it. He threw his spare shirts over his boots and lay down, hidden beside the pick. He remained quite awake. The night wore on, and the candle burnt out. He thought he might be mistaken about No-Hands intentions, but soon after the thought flitted through his mind, he detected a faint glow. He held still and breathed quiet as a cat as the light grew. Shadows danced upon the wall as the lantern swung through the door frame. Skarde heard no footstep, and the shadows about the room raised as the lantern was lowered with stealth that impressed him. Skarde tensed, ready to pounce if No-Hands suddenly loomed over him. A moment later, there was a series of three heavy thuds.

"Curse the dog!" No-Hands spat.

Skarde leapt to his feet, his pick in hand. "Curse him all you wish," he said, "but you won't kick him!"

No-Hands spun about, his eyes wide. On his right hand, in place of a hook he wielded a truncheon. He held it between them defensively.

"So, you sought to crush my skull while I slept in bed unarmed?" Skarde held the pick high. "You filthy coward. I am neither asleep nor weaponless."

"Not the coward's way," No-Hands said. "The pragmatic way of the assassin, in which I've had some practice!"

With one smooth motion, No-Hands slid open a lid on the knob of the bracer of his right wrist with the hook on his left, revealing a small compartment. He snapped his eyes shut tight and struck his left bracer over the right with some force. It sparked like flint on steel, and a crackling brilliant flash burst between them.

Skarde cried out as the sudden brilliance blinded him. In an instant, Skarde sprang upon his chest and a bone cracking blow struck his arm. It might have been his skull.

"Thunir's Axe!" Skarde bellowed, and he rushed forward, swinging his pick wildly.

Skarde blinked and saw a dark shape in front of him. It swung down at him, and he batted something wooden out of the air. No-Hands cried out. Skarde forced his eyes open and, half blind, he did not see anyone near him. Outside his cell, he heard hurrying feet. Skarde ran after his assailant. No-Hands had a lead, and Skarde gave chase, but his injured feet did not suffice. In a moment, No-Hands would be lost in the darkness. A more civilized man might have considered throwing his only weapon too risky an option. Skarde's savage instinct chose in an instant to lash out. He raised the pick above his head and hurled it at the back of his would-be murderer. It flew through the air and landed with a crunch upon No-Hands head.

No-Hands dropped to the ground, face first, and moved no more.

Skarde padded quickly but silently over him. No-Hands was indeed dead. He was in the main concourse, and in the very dim light of a single, far-off torch. He crouched beside the corpse for a long minute, listening and scanning the gloom intently. *I needn't be caught like this*, he thought. *It will bring up awkward questions.*

To his wonder, no-one came to investigate the din. He padded back to his cell and retrieved his pick and No-Hand's lantern. He carried them back to the body. There, he slung No-Hands limp form over his shoulders and delved into the darkness with pick and lantern in hand.

He grumbled as he passed through the abandoned areas of the mine. "No good inns are to be had in these parts, and sleep is hard to come by!"

He moved aside the shuttered planks and made his way at length to the bubble-like cavern. Without ceremony, he tossed No-Hands into the black pit and heard a heavy thud.

"Did you die in battle, or running from your foe?" Skarde said. "Tell your gods what you will. It is no longer a concern of mine."

As he returned, he pondered the flash that had blinded him. Never had he seen a fighting man use such a device. He had seen such a trick performed by a charlatan-priest long ago when he was a green campaigner. He was then much impressed, but still wary of the priest's claims of supernatural power. Since then, he had caught sight of such a trick among a travelling troupe of acrobats and tale tellers. How it worked, he knew not, but he doubted that the players called on otherworldly aid for jests. Skarde pondered No-Hands claim of experience as an assassin. *I hope that there are no more of his old acquaintances about, or I will sleep even less easy.*

Skarde returned to his cell, and after hiding the lantern in his trunk he slept through what was left of the night, though with one eye open. Waking at the bell, he right away sped off to his work area to deposit the pick. He had survived the night. He broke fast with the other bullies, and all remarked on No-Hands absence. Skarde shrugged, stuffed his mouth, and returned to his work. An hour or so had passed after lunch break when Absi appeared, flanked by two swordsmen in scale mail. Skarde, and all his crew, turned to watch the approaching trio.

"Good day, Wrinkles. I have not seen you make rounds before," Skarde said.

Absi glared at him suspiciously. "No-Hands has not reported for duty, nor been seen all day. Do you know aught of this?"

Skarde shrugged. "Perhaps he shirks his duty. No doubt you will find him laying about."

"It is unlike him," Absi retorted, "and there is no way out of the mines without my knowing and my key."

"I expect nothing will escape your keen eyes, Wrinkles, but I know naught of this matter. Good fortune on finding your wayward bully."

"I will uncover the truth," Absi said.

Skarde held his gaze. Absi muttered and shuffled along, taking the swordsmen with him. The slaves gawked at them as they left, and turned back to Skarde. Skarde ignored the lot of them and strode down the center of the cavern aloof and inspecting what work had been done for the day.

"Nothing to be concerned about," he said at last turning about and feigning surprise at his men's gaze. "No-Hands is beyond our concern. Back to work, mind you."

The men looked about at themselves and one by one went back to their labor. Skarde put the issue out of his head as best he could. He had done what he had done, and if No-Hands body was found, it would be found. *And then a fight and an escape*, he thought, *as desperate and hopeless as it may be*. At last, the bell rang to signal the end of the day, and Skarde headed back to his cell. His senses tingled that something was amiss long before he reached it. As he neared it, he saw light and shadows moving and men conversing in low tones inside. His hand reached for the pommel of his sword and felt nothing. He pursed his lips and strode to the doorway. In his cell, were the two swordsmen and Absi.

"Good evening, Ever-Chained," Absi said.

Skarde scowled at the name but said nothing. "Aye. Welcome to my cell."

"We were not successful in locating No-Hands," Absi said.

"What unhappy news," Skarde said.

"Indeed. None have seen him since last eve. Some have said they heard some noises in the night in the main concourse. What did you hear? You are closest to it."

"I slept like a bear. If there were any tussles to be heard, they did not prick my ears."

"Hmm," Absi said. "Some say that you and No-Hands might have come to blows, some say that you argued. Is that so?" Absi's eyes glittered as if he would penetrate into Skarde's skull.

"Aye," said Skarde. "It was I that cut his hands from his wrists, but I did not know him so well back then."

The swordsmen both raised their eyebrows and glanced at each other. Whether this was to hold back laughter or to express disbelief at his flippant tone, Skarde could not say. Absi, conversely, looked on coldly. He walked over to Skarde's chest and opened it. He pulled from its contents the lantern he had taken from No-Hands. Doubt tightened Skarde's stomach. His legs tensed, ready to pounce on the swordsman on his right if need demanded it.

"How did you come by No-Hands lantern?" Absi asked.

"Is that his?" Skarde said. "Tis but a work lantern I have used in the mines."

"This lantern has a copper top with engravings, see?" Absi turned the cap to him, and Skarde could indeed see fine engravings. "No-Hands spoke of the beautiful handiwork this lantern had for such rough use, and his remarks I have not forgotten. What say you?"

"Absi, you put much stock in a lantern."

"Will you not tell me what happened to him?"

Skarde shook his head and met Absi's stare with his own.

"Then I must arrest you on suspicion of murder and keep you in the stock."

Skarde considered his odds in a flash. He would fight unarmed against three sword-wielding men, escape the mines, and flee through an underground citadel into an unwelcoming jungle. Then, he alone might commandeer a ship and sail to freedom. He sighed. He nodded at Absi, accepting his judgement… and time to wait for a better prospect.

They marched him from his cell. The gate room was stocked full of ores awaiting hauling to wherever they were smelted. Skarde wondered at the amount, and what size of army Gul-Zagar planned to equip. Absi unlocked the mine gates, and the trio marched Skarde through the upper halls and finally to the same gaol he had found himself in when he was captured. Absi gestured for Skarde to enter, and he did so. As the heavy wood door closed, Skarde let out a laugh.

"What's so amusing," Absi asked.

"It just occurred to me that in this prison, I am closer to the Sun and sky than I have been in weeks."

Chapter Twelve

She stood above him like a shimmering goddess. Crackling torchlight glistened off her muscled skin like a red moon on water. She was framed by wings of silver tendrils. Coils of silver and black silk streamed from silver and pewter bracers, shaped like wings and studded with pale gems. Upon her head, she wore a crest like a beaked moth's crown, silver and dainty. No other garments she wore. The gaoler stood behind her, mundane in comparison in his red tabard, one hand on his sword pommel, the other bearing a torch. Skarde looked up from his resting place upon her and held her long in his brash gaze.

"You are the woman in the fire," he said.

Sulmei held up her arm in a gesture, glancing to the soldier behind her. "Leave us," she said.

"Your safety, lady," he said.

She stood steady, not saying a word. The man handed the torch to her and left. Skarde heard his mail rustle, and footsteps carry him away. She stood still listening as well, and when there was silence, she turned toward him again.

"You come to the most dismal places adorned more for grand rites in temples or the festivals of decadent aristocrats," Skarde said.

"Gul-Zagar fashions these himself. How? I know not. I would not offend him by spurning his gifts."

"But you do relish the spectacle," Skarde said. It was not a question.

"I do," Sulmei said. "Are you not more concerned with your own plight?"

"I most certainly am, *lady*," he said with a scornful tone, standing to look down at her. "More, I wish to know about what you want. Why are you here? Not just in this dark prison, but on this accursed isle. Our paths cross, but not by chance. Why else would you come? You have plenty of playthings, or so I've heard, and there is little else I could give you – given my current lodgings."

Sulmei's dispassionate mask slipped. Her lips tightened and her brows furrowed. For a moment, she looked more like a frightened girl than a daemonic or divine spirit.

"Who are you?" Skarde said.

"I am Sulmei," she said. "My story is long in telling, and we are short on time. Suffice to say I fled my homeland far to the south where the stars are different. I sailed with freebooters and came to the Temple of Coemis in Byzerdamen."

"The Temple of Coemis?" Skarde said. "An infamous whorehouse in a city notorious for its corrupt civilization?"

Sulmei raised her eyebrows at him. "Would you lecture me like a sniffing priest of virtuous pandering?

Skarde laughed. "Not I. Go on."

"I could go on to tell tales to make your savage ears burn up," she said. "I will only say that there I uncovered a secret power in myself, and for reasons too lengthy to expound upon, I must needs departed. For a brief moment, I was even High Priestess."

Skarde smiled as pride flashed across her face.

"I sought thereafter for knowledge of mystics and wise men. Alas, charlatans and fools were easier to come by, but I found some morsels of knowledge. Of late, I heard of a great sorcerer upon a far-off isle. Yes, I see insight in your eyes, Skarde. I speak of Gul-Zagar."

"And he has taught you the black arts you sought." Skarde said.

"Not all the arts are evil," Sulmei said.

Skarde raised an eyebrow. "What of Gul-Zagar?"

Sulmei's eyes widened, and she glanced down the corridor. "He is persuasive, indeed, like no man I have met. At first, I believed him beyond concerns of good and evil. He believes in his purpose wholly, and he sweeps men up in the net of his convictions too. I assisted him in his work for a promise of instruction in the art of sorcery. He taught me some fundamentals; child's work to him but revelations to me, and so far beyond the metaphysical mummery of the imposters I had crossed before."

"So," Skarde said. He paused for a moment, collecting his thought. "You have what you want. I suspect you are here to taunt me as a scorned paramour."

"Do not think I have come here to play a star-struck girl's games!" She roared, gesturing her censure, her wings of silver and black silk fluttering. Her eyes flashed suddenly with anger and a hint of fear. "I come in need, and you, it is apparent, are in more desperate straits than I am."

"You are an enigma!" Skarde said angrily. He cared not to be chastised by a maiden. He held his hand up for her silence and paced the small space. "Funir's wing! I must begone from these stifling walls and set the wind to my face!"

"Well," Sulmei said in a sigh of relief. "At least you have answered one of my questions."

"What?"

"That you wished to escape," Sulmei said.

"Of course, girl!"

"This I believed when you defeated Gul-Zagar's champion and joined the brotherhood, that you swore an oath only to bide your time."

"So, you think me a faithless oath-breaker?"

Sulmei stared at him with hard eyes, not in a pique of fluster, but with a power of authority that belied her youthful face. "Stay your complaints for a moment, man! In the ears of reasonable men and perhaps the Gods an oath sworn to a captor is set against a pebble. I would not hold you to it. Yet when Toran trained you, it seemed your reluctance was put aside. Eagerly you applied yourself."

"Aye, and I learned much after I swallowed an ounce of my pride. Yet was I rewarded? Tossed into the mines, no better off than a slave!"

"I despaired," Sulmei said. "I saw that your fervor for swordplay eclipsed your purpose of freedom. Of all the men here, you alone seemed fitting for the task I had need of. Now that I know you wish to escape, my hope rises again. Would you now swear to fight with me? You will not escape without my help, and without you..."

Sulmei's eyes glistened. She turned away from Skarde and steadied herself.

"Without you, I will be worse than dead, and the bell shall toll all too soon."

Skarde stood silent for a moment. His jaw clenched. "There is much to consider. You have not told me half of what is going on here, I'll wager, and a man could mull your words for a month..."

"I will be doomed by then," Sulmei said. She turned back to him. Her eyes did not plead.

"Aye. Needs must when devils wield the whip. So let us swear an oath, and fight until we die!"

Her eyes were like fire, and her bosom heaved. She answered him with a kiss, rushing into his arms and holding him tight. Skarde glanced at the open cell door, but soon forgot the gaoler. Such was her passion he forgot all but the softness of her lips and the heat of her body. What trust he might place in her was thought for another time, but at length his mind wandered back to practical concerns.

"There is the matter of my imprisonment," he said at last.

She laughed softly at his side, as if his words were foolish. "Come," she said, standing and tugging on his arm with surprising strength.

Skarde stood and fitted back his clothing as she picked up the sputtering brand.

"You did not answer my first question," he said gazing at the orange tongues licking from the torch. "Are you the woman in the fire?"

She gazed at him for a long moment, her eyes searching his for trust. She lifted the flame before her and held her right hand beside it. Skarde's eyes widened as she slid her naked flesh into the flame. He expected her to let the flame only just kiss her hand and remove it, but she held it steady, fire on flesh, and held his eyes without the slightest sign of distress.

"Hodan's beard," he whispered.

"Come," she said, the flames still dancing through her fingers. "We've tarried overlong."

She turned and took a stride out of the cell with rolling hips. Skarde took a step toward the door and looked cautiously out. He had not planned an escape, and neither did the gaoler. He would rather not have a sword sticking through him. He followed her, and she banged a fist on the heavy wooden door at the end of the short hall of cells. It opened, and the gaoler's eyes went wide. He stepped back and drew his sword.

"Back in your cell, brute!" he yelled.

Sulmei stepped through the portal, his blade a foot from her bare chest, and lifted her arms. Her wings spread wide, and the gaoler looked on agape.

"Sheathe your weapon, warrior," she said. Her voice dripped with honey. "Skarde is a prisoner no more. He comes with me."

The gaoler's face softened, yet he looked warily back at Skarde. He nodded at her.

"Yes, your ladyship," he said, and he put away his weapon and stood back.

Sulmei continued. Skarde walked past the swordsman and gave him a wily grin. "Whatever comes of this madness, I am enjoying this hour," he said to her.

They went directly to the mines. It was a bitter path, treading from one prison to a deeper one, but the spark of hope in Skarde's heart now lit a fire.

"I know a little of your plight, Skarde," Sulmei spoke as they walked. She was careful to speak low, and only when no one was about. "But tell me the truth, for we must prepare. Is No-Hands dead?"

"Aye," Skarde said, and he relayed the events of the previous night to her in blunt, plain speech.

"An assassin!" she said, remarking on the flash powder he used. "You pick your enemies well. I know the caves thoroughly. I will take care of his remains today before it is discovered. Follow my lead when we reach the mines."

Soon the large double doors of the mine loomed above them. Sulmei indicated that he should knock, and he pounded upon them with a closed fist. In short time, Wrinkles appeared at the barred window to his chancery.

"What the devil!" He spat looking down at Skarde, beside Sulmei.

"Open the mine doors, Absi," Sulmei commanded. "I will not crane my neck to address you."

Wrinkles stared down at the pair, his brows knotted with suspicion. Before Sulmei could speak further, he disappeared. Skarde shifted impatiently, glancing over at Sulmei, wondering again how enticing, yet so out of place she seemed. A key clacked in the doors, and they creaked inward. Sulmei strode forward without so much as a glance at Absi. Skarde's eyes flashed in amusement, and he came next.

"Lady!" Absi said, his voice rose and fell. "I really must ask what circumstance brings you, and *he*, here!"

Sulmei stood in the center of the gate room shimmering in the light. Old Absi was not so old that he was not stirred to gaze on lustily. She lifted her wings high in the air and turned to inspect the room. Even Skarde rubbed his eyes, wondering if he were glamoured.

"You have provided such bounty for The Master's forges, Absi. You shall be rewarded," she said, her tone changed considerably.

"Aye... ah, the ore!" Absi said. "Thank you, ladyship. We have struck fertile veins." He laughed, pleased at the praise. "There is the matter, lady, of..." he said, gesturing at Skarde.

"I have learned of the matter," Sulmei said, "And I thank you for your swift and diligent action. You are, however, unaware of the details, which Skarde has commendably kept silent, as I have asked him. Do we have privacy?"

Absi looked hither and thither in the passages beyond the mine gate and shut them. "Aye, Lady. No one about now."

"Then I shall advise you as needed. Skarde and your most admirable officer No-Hands have I tasked with the finding of a particular gem. Based upon my divinations, it must be deep in the heart of the mountain. Skarde and No-Hands delved into the abandoned mines and who knows what caves beyond. What became of No-Hands I do not know, but Skarde is innocent of any wrongdoing. He and Peg-Leg will convene to find No-Hands, if they might, and complete my task."

"Is... is this The Master's wish?" Absi asked.

"I serve The Master," Sulmei said approaching him. "I ask you give them some leave to do this. Our aims are swiftly coming to fruition. I would be most grateful for this, and if you would seal your lips in this matter."

"Aye," Absi said. "I will do this."

"My thanks, wise Absi," she said.

She turned and her wings spread as if she were a creature of flight as she moved into the deeper caves. Skarde nodded at Absi as he passed him, but his eyes were on Sulmei alone. Skarde's long strides took him past her before they reached the main concourse. He was vexed to see four slaves and a bully in the large chamber, for they looked at him with surprise and suspicion. When Sulmei emerged from the tunnel behind him, they looked on agog. Sulmei gave them a cool glance, and the two continued to Skarde's cell. Once there, Sulmei spared no time and undid Skarde's belt.

"What are you doing?" Skarde said.

"Isn't it clear?" she said, tugging down his breeches. "Are you tired?"

"Of course not!" Skarde said, offended. "But we have plans to lay."

"My visit will attract attention, as seldom have I visited the mines. Make love to me again. It is what they will expect, and their curiosity be satisfied to hear the whispers of lovers and not conspirators."

Skarde looked at her with furrowed eyes. She pushed him with her considerable strength, but he outmatched her and stood.

"And also, I desire it. If things go ill, it may be our last embrace," she spoke more softly.

He took her hand, and at once she pushed him again. He fell to his bed, and she mounted him. She gasped aloud as they gripped each other.

"Do not be silent," she said.

"Oh!" he said mildly.

"You wag your tongue enough betimes," she said. "Now it is needed."

"Ahhhh!" he yelled.

"Aye!" she moaned, dramatically. "That is better!"

Skarde slapped her rump unkindly, and she yowled back. She looked at him not with anger, but delight.

"You are a rare woman, Sulmei."

"Aye," and that is why I am here she spoke softly. "Gul-Zagar employs me in the art of making his swords."

"Does not Mor, the giant, make the swords?"

Sulmei gasped, both at their lovemaking and the revelation. "You know his name. You impress me, savage!" she spoke more loudly.

"I heard the name as... it seemed... you attempted to seduce him."

Sulmei laughed. "I've no other way but my wiles to ply him for his secrets, and no way to harm him. Pah! He is grim and haughty. Do not be jealous, Skarde!"

"Aye," Skarde said.

"He forges swords as no man can. These, however, are not swords of steel, but a mystic element Gul-Zagar provides. Some of his ancient race once worked this metal, but it is beyond even his power to forge. He needs the heat of the deep earth for a hearth."

"And what of you?" Skarde said.

"I am, for lack of a more impressive term, his bellows. Even the heat of molten rock is not enough to forge this metal. I can purify and strengthen the fire, so it burns hotter than bolts from the sky or a dragon's breath. Only with my fire, Mor's might, and Gul-Zagar's eldritch power have we made these swords."

Skarde closed his eyes. The pleasure of Sulmei's body made thoughts of other things difficult.

"Gul-Zagar has withheld much, and I have been unable to study much of sorcery. But, I have learned some things from the writing of The Master's long dead people. Strange were they, and sinister. Their powers were great and subtle. I have come to think that I did not discover The Master, but that he lured me in subtle ways here for this purpose."

"But why spend so much effort on a few swords?" he said. "Even the finest sword cannot overcome an army."

"They are fine swords forsooth, but much more. They have wills of their own. When the first of these were made, he summoned the spirit of an enemy of his own. From across the howling depths of time, it came. Not human, not anymore, but a loathsome *thing*, and he trapped it in the sword."

As Skarde listen, he felt her horror, and his hair stood on end.

"I will not speak of the others now, save the sixth, just now made..." She shut her eyes and ceased rocking her hips over his.

He also shut his eyes. He could feel Sulmei atop him. Her flesh, her blood pumping through her veins, the depth of her heart. All shared. One being. Then, an image came to Skarde's mind of a young man. He could not quite see the features of his face, but knew, somehow that his eyes were brown and studious, his hair blonde. Tall and proud he stood unmoving. But he was trapped, and now in mortal danger. Skarde... Sulmei... desired to liberate him, to shield him. His skin froze. His doom was beyond his grasp, and a blade pierced his chest. Like a demon, the blade howled and drank deep.

Skarde howled also.

"He was a prince!" Sulmei growled, as if she shared his vision. "The rightful heir of Nurména, whose black-hearted cousin now sits on his throne. He was accounted wise beyond his years and sagely."

"This is a dark art!" Skarde said.

"Indeed. I can only now guess what powers they might imbue on the weapon. Which leads me to my fate and the danger I am in."

She let out a growl. Skarde gripped her thighs as she galloped forward.

"I discovered that the last sword is to house a spirit of fire. Gul-Zagar advised me that Mor would serve as sacrifice for this. His mighty soul should inhabit the blade and be lord over all others. A liar!" she moaned, and she bent to kiss Skarde.

"It was my fire he wanted all along. Not just to forge his swords, but to take my sorcery that can increase and diminish pain and pleasure, share thoughts and desires, to sway all the others... the flame of the mind... and so sway their wielders! I am to be the sacrifice!" Sulmei let out a rolling cry.

They gripped at each other. They fell together in the rough bed and held each other. Skarde listened to her breathing and felt her strong heart beating in her flesh upon his fingertips.

"You have told me enough to chew on for some time," he said at last. "Yet we still have not devised a plan of escape."

She traced her fingers along his arms and chest. "I will arrange for a route of escape. We may pass the great doors near the forge chamber and move quickly through the citadel. The dockyard is now built, and I have friendly relations with a captain among the reavers. There, we can board a ship and sail before anything is accounted amiss. When Gul-Zagar's plans for the seventh sword are foiled, his need for me will be ended. I do not think he will bother to pursue us. His heart is as cold as a winter stone, and I wager he will rather pursue some further scheme than us."

"And what of Mor?" Skarde said.

Sulmei looked into his eyes. "I thought you understood your place in the plan. Perhaps I must be plainer. You will kill the giant."

Chapter Thirteen

"What!" Skarde jumped out of bed, looking down upon her.

She smiled and traced her fingertips over her hips casually. "What did you think your part would be?"

"To slay mortal men hindering our escape, not battle a fiend summoned from the mists of legend!"

"Quiet your voice," Sulmei whispered. "Who knows what ears bend our way."

"Your confidence in me is stirring," Skarde said, "and quite mad. I do not even have a sword!"

"Mor shall make you one! Come," Sulmei said stern but quiet. "Come to my arms and speak in lover's murmurs."

Skarde stared at her amazed for a long moment. She gestured again, and he lay beside her, holding her body. She stroked his blonde hair and smiled.

"When you seemed content to remain with the Brotherhood of Iron, I sought out others who might champion me, but none are your equal. I did not expect any of them to battle Mor like a gladiator in a pit, nor would I expect you to do so either. There is time to prepare some plan. As for the sword, the seventh and last of these blades, swords that will someday be accounted legends, will be yours. The blade craves for a soul, like the first breath of a newborn, and until it breathes one in, I will be in deadly danger. Mor, too, is a spirit of fire. One deep bite, and the sorcery of the blade will rip his spirit from its moorings."

Skarde laughed.

Sulmei crossed her brows. "What amuses you?"

"My charming girl," he said. "We are all most likely to die in this plan. I like it."

Sulmei shook her head. "I find you strange, Skarde."

"Mad," he said. "Mad in a mad world."

Skarde worked diligently in his part of the mine for several days. He had much to think about. His men watched him with wide eyes, and the bullies also whispered. Before the end of work bell rang on the third day, Tarsazi approached him, and looked at him sheepish.

"Is it true?" he said. "Did you lie with The Master's priestess?"

"Priestess, is she? I suppose you are right. Others have called her a witch... among other things."

"Oh," he lowered his eyes. "I mean no disrespect!"

"No, Tarsazi. I am not angered. You and the others talk, and there is no news, or tales, or diversions to be had in this Tartarean gloom."

"No indeed," he said.

"Would you be free, Tarsazi?"

Tarsazi's eyes widened in fear. "I... I work and serve!"

"No need for that, man. You asked me a question, and I answer plain. I laid with her. A civil man might balk at answering such a question, but I am not civil. Nor are her appetites known only to a few. Tarsazi, I would taste freedom. Would you?"

Tarsazi looked uneasily at his face, and seeing Skarde was solemn, he straightened his back. "I suppose few men would choose the mines over the lives they once had."

"What of a life you could have, uncertain though it may be. Would you fight for freedom?"

"I was never a soldier," Tarsazi said. He glanced over his shoulder and lowered his voice. "I have won a few barehanded brawls, though."

Skarde smiled. "That's a start, man! Do you think any of the others might be keen on a little adventure? They may speak more freely to you than to I."

"Mayhap," Tarsazi said.

"Well, test their tempers but be not too blunt. I have a sharp tongue poorly suited for subtlety. You will do better."

Just then, as if their conversation queued an entrance, Skarde and Tarsazi both turned their heads to the entrance to the cave. A regular tapping announced Peg-Leg, and in moments, he briefly looked in and motioned for Skarde to follow him. Right away, he stepped back into the tunnels. Skarde raised an eyebrow Tarsazi's way and headed toward the exit. He heard a quiet tapping as he rounded the mouth of the cave. Peg-Leg was making his way down the tunnel, bearing a torch. Skarde caught up with him in a few long strides.

"You should not have come like this," Skarde said. "Better to send a slave if you want to relay a message. Our movements are marked, no doubt. Curse these intrigues."

"Sulmei let me know of the plan being yet devised. You tarry overlong!" Peg-Leg said. "The sands of her hourglass pour out, and you have done nothing!"

"Has she sent you to mark my headway?" Skarde said.

"I spoke to her the same day she came to you. I have come on my own to see you do not fail in your pledge to her," Peg-Leg said.

Skarde smiled. Peg-Leg was only a little younger than himself, and clearly, or so Skarde thought, besotted with her. *Am I, also, under her spell,* he wondered. *This plan is madness.*

"Why do you leer at me so?" Peg-Leg said.

"Come," Skarde said walking on. "Since you are here, let us make full use of our heads. The more often we put them together, the more Absi will look in on us."

"Where are you going?" Peg-Leg said, tapping along loudly.

Skarde slowed his pace. "Try your best to quiet your footsteps. As for my tarrying – have you seen the cyclopean foe I have been asked to best?"

"Does your heart falter?" Peg-Leg said.

Skarde shot him a hard look. "If I did not know you were a decent sort, and fecklessly in love, I would run you through for that insult. I would... if I had my sword. We have little to work with and a mighty challenge ahead. How might our plan be achieved with any chance of success? What will we need to do it, and how might we keep prying eyes from unearthing our plot? How so, Peg-Leg?"

"Not by idleness," Peg-Leg said.

"I have spent days pondering these problems. I need your help, not bickering."

"I fret for her life. Very well. Let us not quarrel."

They passed a tunnel, close to the main concourse, and Skarde held up his finger to quiet his companion. Carefully, they tread forward, and it seemed they evaded notice. They delved into the abandoned mines, and soon came to the boarded passage.

"Here is where I sought the noise of Mor's hammering. No-Hands followed and ambushed me. Come, I will show you the path we must take."

Skarde pulled aside the loose boards, and they entered. In short order they came to the bubble chamber that No-Hands pushed him into. He looked down and his eyes widened.

"Funir's Wing! There is naught but scorches and ash down there. Could that be Sulmei's work?"

"Aye, it could be. She acts faster than we do."

"No-Hands shoved me, most cowardly, from behind here. He left me to die. I discovered a crack and opened it enough to press through, which led after some struggle to a cavern where Mor forges amid a great pool of lava," Skarde said.

"Aye," said Peg-Leg.

"At one end, there is the giant's lair, and a gate by which Sulmei comes and goes I believe."

"She does. Only Mor can open it."

"I guessed right, then. I escaped the other way, where the lava pool laps around a corner and leads to a long hall, which, I discovered later, can be reached from the ledge over the lava pool. In that tunnel there is a crack over another round chamber. Here is where my plan lies."

"I know not of this place," Peg-Leg said. "Can you show it to me?"

"Nay, not without risking death or discovery. We will need rope, hammers, and pitons to reach it without certain hurt. More rope will be needed to escape, for the exit I found opens to a hole in the ceiling of Grim-Face's area.

"That is well. If any of the Brotherhood in the mines besides us can be trusted to help Sulmei's cause, it is he."

"Good. We will need all the luck we can find," Skarde said. "My hope is to lead Mor over this chamber. We must weaken its roof, so that when the giant steps on it, he will fall in. Maybe then he will be injured. I trust it not to kill him, but so long as he is in that trap, I will have some distant hope in Hell in landing a blow on him. We must get five or six valiant men down there to assist us to score away at its edges and so prepare it."

Peg-Leg's eyes narrowed as Skarde spoke, and he shook his head. "No, Skarde. We must do it ourselves somehow. We cannot involve the slaves. Too many ears and too many mouths."

"Some must know," Skarde said. "When the time comes to fight, they must be prepared."

"What fight? We shall escape by stealth and speed."

"There may be more fighting than you expect. Besides, I could not leave Belgeti and my own men to slavery without a chance even to fight," Skarde said.

"No," Peg-Leg said, his voice rising. "They are good men, but I shall not have my lady imperiled!"

"Yea or nay, she is imperiled. As are we all. I have already spoken to some of an uprising. Too late for cloak-and-dagger."

Peg-Leg turned and paced away, clacking angrily. He let out a roar and punched the air. "You should have consulted me first, fool! My lady..."

"She is not your lady!" Skarde shouted. "Her name is scarlet! Be your eyes open? You are in love or bewitched."

Peg-Leg lunged at him and threw a punch. He dodged aside, but the strike was quick and caught Skarde on the chin. He moved away from the hole, and Peg-Leg threw blow after blow. Skarde grunted in pain. He was a brawler like him, though not as strong. Skarde slapped his neck and almost toppled him, but

Peg-Leg returned fast and grappled him. They both fell to the stony ground.

"Best vent your wrath now," Skarde said, and he almost lost a tooth for it.

Tired of the outburst, Skarde growled and sought to pin Peg-Leg. Skarde topped him at last, though he still struggled.

"This does not help her cause!" Skarde said.

At that, Peg-Leg's struggle lessened. "You will speak of Sulmei with respect," he spat.

Skarde shook his head. "No disrespect. I only speak the truth as I see it. Quit your struggle! Your demand is fair. Lady Sulmei would best be served by us both."

Their grips upon each other lessened tentatively, and at last Skarde stood.

"I'm not blind," Peg-Leg said. "I know her inclinations. We cannot judge her, for she is set apart from the likes of us. Her place is among the seekers of hidden lore and powers beyond mortal ken."

"No doubt. But let's get off this damned island before we argue more."

Skarde offered his hand to pull Peg-Leg up, but he stood on his own.

"Agreed," he said.

Skarde and Peg-Leg made their way back to the mines. They debated the details of their plan. Peg-Leg would get the rope, the pitons, and the hammers, though a few could be found already among their men. Skarde would ask among the slaves their desire to leave and their desire to fight. Peg-Leg balked at this, and predicted ruination would come of it, but as it was too late, he merely demanded caution. They agreed it would be best to find five or six strong and able slaves to descend into the bowels of the volcano with Skarde as their guide. They would take with them several days rations, and work on sapping the roof of the chamber which was to be Mor's grave. Peg-Leg advised this work should go on as Mor forged the last sword. His thunder would cover their own clamor, or so they hoped. Also, a few missing slaves from each team might go unnoticed.

Skarde was pleased when Tarsazi approached him the next day. Several of the lads would fight, and those that were unwilling to fight at least seemed eager to escape. He believed none would betray them. Skarde was taken aback that the whole crew was in the know. *Perhaps Peg-Leg had a point*, he thought, *but too late for laments now*. Skarde asked Tarsazi to make sure that all held their tongues tight.

Skarde delayed his plan to ask Grim-Face's view on rebellion, until he could speak with Peg-Leg to share news and progress. That next morning, as his crew began their labors Skarde felt an unease, a throbbing in his feet, and then a faint rumble deep in the earth. *Mor's hammer falls again. The last sword is being forged.*

Skarde walked to the end of his cavern and stood facing the dark tunnels. He turned back, thinking better of another direct, possibly suspicious, meeting with Peg-Leg. He gritted his teeth and managed his men – work kept his mind at peace. Not long after, Belgeti appeared. Skarde saw him as he chatted and laughed with his men.

"Belgeti!" Skarde said, smiling.

"Master," Belgeti said with a bow.

Skarde laughed. "Come, let's make a tour of the tunnels and make sure they are straight."

Grabbing a torch, the two wandered into the darkness 'til they found as reclusive an alcove as they could manage.

"What news?" Skarde whispered. Hidden as they were, sound carried too easily in the stony passageways.

"Peg-Leg grew restless when he heard the thunder in the earth. Restless as he has not been before," Belgeti said. "He said you could explain his unease. He said also that he will have all the supplies you asked for in a week, but they must be taken away that day." He shrugged.

"Aye, good. Things are moving swiftly now. Are you still willing to fight?"

Belgeti smiled. "Would I lay down and bring shame to my ancestors? Of course, I fight!"

Skarde felt better with Belgeti at his side. "That we met in captivity is a shame. I would put my back to yours in battle."

Belgeti bowed his head.

"Have you spoken to the other men? How are their spirits?" Skarde asked.

"Peg-Leg is ill at ease about that, too. We will all fight."

"Haha! A worthy lot," Skarde said. "Some of mine will fight also. Tell Peg-Leg I see the wit of his concern. Let us recruit no more to our cause 'til the hour is upon us, though I will speak with Grim-Face. He might see our comings and goings. Let us put his wonder to rest and hope he will ally with us."

"I'm sure he will. He has spoken in open discontent, or so I have heard."

"Now," Skarde said. "Let me lay down my plan, plain for you to hear. We shall kill the giant."

Belgeti smiled but looked at Skarde wide-eyed. "My people say, drink with friends at the campfire, not in the saddle. Kill a giant? What do you mean?"

Skarde laughed. "Think me a drunk if you will. That is how I got into this mess. Yet, that is our plan."

"Myself and a few of my riders could kill this Mor in the open plains. He may be a hundred times as strong as a man, but a hundred arrows can be hurled in moments."

"That would be a sight," Skarde smiled. "I must start afresh in my thinking about the bow. Alas, we have not bows, or horses, or plains to ride on. We must kill him in the tunnels. Sulmei will provide to me the sword, and I shall kill Mor."

"Ha, you *are* drunk!"

"Reckless no doubt, but not drunk," Skarde said. He outlined the plan he and Peg-Leg had come up with.

Belgeti shook his head. "There is much wisdom of war in the sayings of my people. Some speak for your plan, others against, but that seems a desperate hope."

"Aye. Toran taught the sayings of the war-philosopher Harquan, and some goes both for and against. I do not think there is much choice but to fight, and if you have a better plan, I would hear it!"

Belgeti shrugged. "To the Hells. Let's do it."

Skarde smiled. "I plan on leading you down there with picks, pitons, ropes, ladders, and food. You shall oversee the men. Weaken the floor as your gut guides you. Work only when Mor does, and may his thunder cover your racket. We hope your absence will not be noticed over a few days. When done, remain down there, or higher up in the passages until the time comes.

"I should bring bedrolls also!" Belgeti said.

Chapter Fourteen

When Mor's thunder rolled through the ground, Skarde felt uneasy. It was like a drum of war, but a call he could not yet answer. *The wait is worse than the battle*, he thought. *Damn this endless lingering.* Days passed, and the faint pounding continued. He had half a mind to go into the depths and take an account of things himself despite the risks. At night, he dreamt of voyages never completed, of losing something important, of time wasted.

"I'll go mad," he said to Tarsazi. "Visions haunt me and prompt me to do things I know well I need to do."

"And my stomach tightens as the hour approaches," Tarsazi said. "I wonder if I will die."

Skarde's eyes raised in concern, but also in pity. "Don't speak of such things. You'll spook yourself, or worse, the others. When it happens, just fight, and know that your bondage is at an end, one way or another."

Tarsazi smiled nervously and went back to work.

One morning, not long after the work bell, Belgeti came and told him that word had come from Sulmei.

"Six days after this, and the sword will be complete. You must be on the ledge and awaiting her move," Belgeti said.

Skarde recalled the terrible heat. "I must bring water skins. Aye, tell Peg-Leg to have his chosen men awaiting me tonight in secrecy at the third fork following the main concourse, with all the supplies we agreed upon."

Belgeti held his fist over his chest and left. Now, an eagerness set upon Skarde's heart.

"A long, slow march now begun, to end in a mad dash. Thunir, if you can see through the stone and darkness, turn your eyes upon us. If not, may the tale come to you on the wings of a storm."

That night, Skarde kept himself awake 'til the taps and shuffles that echoed through the mines turned to eerie silence. Then he stood, taking with him No-Hand's lantern, a sling of four stolen water skins and a pair of thick leather gloves. These things he planned to leave on the ledge for the purpose of holding and cooling a red-hot sword. He knew not Sulmei's exact plan on delivering the sword to him and prepared as best he could. He snuck along the tunnels, quiet as a cat to the place where Tarsazi, and two brothers named Farasid and Kasuk awaited him.

"*Tss*. Tarsazi," Skarde hissed.

Tarsazi stood forward, seeming to emerge from stone, so well was he hid. He motioned and two others appeared beside him. They crept along, silent enough to impress him, 'til they reached the third juncture. Out of the darkness, several men, Skarde's own, emerged. Kasuk gasped, thinking that they had been discovered by the guard, but he kept his composure. They nodded at each other in the dim light and gestured at the packs and supplies. Skarde shouldered his share of the load and more, and the others followed him. The seven reached the shuttered entrance, and Skarde pulled the boards away with his hands. They murmured amongst themselves, but Belgeti shot them severe looks and silenced them with a curt gesture. Only once inside the forbidden tunnels did they speak. They spoke their names and shook hands.

"And these are Aslanbek and Urmag," Belgeti said, introducing two men of Skarde's crew.

They came to the first bubble-like chamber, now decorated only with the ashen remains of the two corpses. Skarde found himself shuddering as they tied off a length of their plentiful supply of rope. *How close I came to a humiliating death in a grave that would be lost 'til the world be destroyed and remade,* he thought. They descended, and Skarde came last. Skarde showed them the gap he had knocked out and struggled through. They followed him, and like worms they descended into the earth. Skarde hushed them, though they made no complaint against the growing heat. They came to the opening to the ledge. Skarde motioned for them to move to the right, and they followed him. As they moved down the tunnel, a hot breeze came up to meet them stirring the otherwise still air. They halted and listened and heard a far-off thud. Hearing nothing else but the churning of lava, Skarde continued. They came to the larger way. On their right were the cooler, dark tunnels and just beyond it the place they would lay their trap. The men all turned their faces leftward, their wide eyes reflecting a red glow. Skarde eyed it with suspicion. *Has the lava advanced? Perhaps it ebbs and flows like water almost frozen in time?* The blackened breaker drew Skarde's eye, its steady surface hinting at movement. Just then, came a calamitous din, and voice boomed about the stone walls.

"Heat the metal!" Mor's voice rumbled through man and stone alike.

The men shot back into the mouth of the hole from which they had come, their eyes wide and their breath held. Mor's hammer rang against the anvil once more, and Skarde thought it best to move them. They were brave, but this unnatural place set even Skarde's teeth on edge. He stalked out into the cavern and looked across the lava for any sign of an approaching giant. Seeing none, he waved them on. They jogged quick but silent to the fragile ground above the bubble chamber. He guided them around it and tied off a length of rope upon a stalagmite, even as Mor began hammering in solemn strokes.

"There is the hole I gazed down," Skarde said pointing. The men gathered round to hear him between the smites. "Beware. Make use of your ladders, pitons, ropes and other supplies as you see fit. Hide and be silent when Mor is not at work. His lair is just beyond his forge. Belgeti... I will show you how to escape here, though you stay for four days 'til I return."

"I would see the giant," Belgeti said.

"It's a risk," Skarde said.

"Aye," Belgeti said. "We all risk our lives here. I would see my foe."

Skarde nodded and led him back up the shaft to the ledge. He motioned Belgeti on, and they crawled on their bellies under the fence. Silently, Skarde removed the bracer of water skins and gloves and laid them aside. He awaited Mor's hammer strokes, and when the deafening knell filled the chamber, they both rose and peered just between the stalagmites. They gazed, frozen in horror by the supernatural sight of Mor's cyclopean form, the lava fall, and Sulmei's glowing body. Belgeti stared wide-eyed for a dozen quick heartbeats. He sunk low in silence, and crawled back to the downward hole, and Skarde came behind him.

"We are beyond the mortal realm, surely," Belgeti said, trembling, as they stood now at the bottom.

"Beyond what men can make good sense of, if nothing else," Skarde said.

"I will stay to do what I must, but the walls seem to close in on me! Show me the way out. A horse lord must know the land, even below it seems."

He led Belgeti past the trap, where the men had already gotten most of the supplies into the chamber. Belgeti had a quick word with Farasid. Skarde took a length of rope and led Belgeti along the slowly turning cavern 'til it led up.

"Here is the hole up which you must crawl to find an opening in Grim-Face's area. I will leave you here unless you want sore knees," Skarde said.

Belgeti shook his head. "Wind in your hair, Sun to your back, Skarde," he said, extending his hand.

Skarde took his arm and gripped him close. He turned and climbed upward. He came to the opening in the ceiling, looped the rope about a rock he hoped would suffice, and lowered himself down, gripping both ends of the rope in his hands. At the bottom, he tugged the untied rope, and it fell down after him. With caution, he returned to his cell to sleep as he could.

Four days hence he awoke just before the work bell rang. Slipping on his boots, he grabbed another brace of water skins he had stolen. At the mess, he wolfed down some victuals and visited his men.

"Work light today," he said.

They nodded but looked at each other with unease. Then Skarde heard Mor's hammer, faint yet clear. His heart quickened.

"Quick thinking today, men," he announced to the cavern.

He grabbed a torch and strode straight to Grim-Face's cavern. At the brink he stood, and caught the bully's eye, and Grim-Face came to meet him.

"What?" Grim-Face said, his voice muffled by the enormous scar that ran down his face, and cleft his lips.

"There will be a battle shortly," Skarde said. "Will you fight for your freedom and your men? Or will you fight to remain in the dark?"

"What?" Grim-Face said, as if Skarde spoke a riddle.

Skarde laid his plan open to Grim-Face in plain language and beseeched his help in battling for freedom. Skarde kept close to Grim-Face – to whisper the last whisper of their plot but also to deny Grim-Face the advantage of the reach of his truncheon if he refused.

Grim-Face gave a muffled laugh. "I fought for the Brotherhood, as you can see. I have been richly rewarded." He gestured from his scarred face to the stone walls. "I will fight with my brothers now, for freedom. What sign should I look for?"

"I'll be dropping in," Skarde said.

Grim-Face looked to the ceiling where the hole was well hidden before Skarde could point it out. He turned back to Skarde, smiled as only he could, and returned to his work. Skarde jogged back to the main concourse and into the abandoned tunnels. He did not see any sign that he had been caught out, but his instincts demanded action. *The swifter this is done, the better*, he thought. For the last time, he pulled open the boards and rather than replacing them quietly, he pulled them off, and threw them down the tunnel.

"Never more!" he cried, and he hurtled forward.

He ran through the shafts, swung down the rope left days ago to the ash-stained chamber, and made his way down to the shelf. *Doom! Doom!* Mor's hammer rang louder. Reaching the ledge, he peered between the fence, and saw the same terrible scene. The sword blazed white-hot, and sparks from Mor's hammer filled the whole chamber. *Soon!* Skarde thought. He dropped his new water skins to the ground. Rushing back, he shuffled down the low tunnel to the cavern below. He stopped for a moment at the bottom to listen for words or any other sign of danger. There, he saw a gleaming gem in a niche in the rough rock, ten paces from the lava pool. Right away, he thought of the ruse Sulmei had told of the magical gem deep in the mountain. *Has the lie come true?*

He approached and examined it. It was on the hilt of a dagger. The hilt and sheath were jeweled gold and silver, wrought into a leering goat's head. A black leather sheath decorated with silver and small gems was of a different maker but equally good quality. *A ceremonial dagger*, Skarde thought. *Gaudy, yet sturdy looking and well-made.* He grabbed the sheath and pulled out the weapon. The design on the hilt slithered over the blade a thumb length, like a lewd tongue. He noticed now that he was sweating, and not just from the heat. *It has an evil feel.* His palms tingled as he slid it back into its sheath and with a sneer, he left it where he found it, wondering if Sulmei had placed it there.

Mor's hammering called Skarde back from his musing. He walked toward the trap. Before he reached it a head poked out of the rock and shadow of the curving wall, and Skarde recognized Tarsazi. He gestured robustly for Skarde to halt. Belgeti appeared and joined him.

"Wait," Belgeti said.

He went to the wall and found footholds, creeping across to Skarde, and never touching the floor.

"I'm not a climber," he chortled, "but I made it! The floor is very weak. We made a break there," he said pointing at a hole, "by accident and Farasid was injured, though he walks."

"The job is done then?" Skarde said.

"Aye. The accident was fortunate enough, as it was close to the wall, and we used it to climb in and out of. We even managed to stand a few pointy stalagmites in there. May Mor impale himself!"

"Good work friend," Skarde said, clapping Belgeti on the back. "No trouble?"

"Aye, trouble. Mor came into the tunnel yesterday, almost to where we stand now. We hid and dared not to move or speak for hours. No matter. We had almost finished our work."

Skarde nodded and stepped closer to look.

"Ayii, careful," Belgeti said. "From here on 'til that hole we made there, a man might or might not break through."

"Thanks, man. It won't be long now. Hide further back and await fire and battle."

Belgeti grinned and laughed to himself, almost eager for what was to come. He climbed back along the stone wall, and Skarde ran back up the way to the ledge. Mor's hammer thundered, and Skarde took a long draw off a freshwater skin before looking over the fence. The giant's hammer ceased falling, and he held the glowing orange-white brand up with tongs to scrutinize. Skarde could see it had a guard, handle, and pommel as one piece. While neither he nor his father was a smith, he knew such a thing was difficult.

"More heat," Mor grumbled.

Sulmei, her flesh only glowing red in parts now, stood stiff as Mor held the blade near her chest. *She fears a sudden strike as her use comes to an end. Brave lass.* She took the radiant blade in her bare hands and plunged it into the lava fall. She closed her eyes and swayed trance-like as the blade and molten rock both grew in brilliance from red to orange, to a painful blue-white. She handed the blazing star back to Mor, who took in back in his tongs.

Skarde slipped back below the line of the fence as Mor hammered on. For nearly two hours he waited as the giant hammered and Sulmei worked her sorcery. He drank his way through a water skin, and another, and wondered if he had brought enough. As he considered peeking out again, Mor's hammering stopped, and there was only the sound of the magma stream.

"Now comes the final quenching of the sword!" Sulmei's voice boomed dramatically.

Skarde wondered if this was part of the ritual, or if she meant only to warn Skarde. He put aside any pondering and put on the leather gloves as quickly as he could. He peered over the fence. Sulmei held the white-hot sword over her head, and a red glow crept down her arm. She stepped across the blackened basalt pathway toward him and stepped out into the lava in her bare feet. She did not sink in as the molten rock turned blackish about her feet and flaked off as she stepped.

"Hodan's beard," he muttered, his eyes wide.

She trod with graceful pomp halfway toward him and thrust the sword into the molten rock. A circle of bright orange spread out from the sword's plunge, and the molten surface bubbled and boiled. She pulled the sword out and swung it in brisk flashing arcs about her. Red-orange molten spatter flew from the blade, and in a practiced sweep, she hurled the blade towards him!

"Hells!" he spat and dodged low.

The burning brand flew over his head and clanged upon the stony wall, landing on the floor near him, illuminating his hidden aerie with ruddy light. He grabbed two of the water skins he had left here days ago and pulled the cap off.

"What is this!" Mor boomed. "Blast thee, mortal fool!"

Skarde took no mind and doused the handle first, squeezing the skin with all haste. He cursed as the water sputtered off the searing metal. Boiling droplets stung his skin and steam almost broiled his arms. He opened the second, and poured it over the length of the blade, gritting his teeth against the pain. Vapor hissed up around him. He had hardly emptied the second skin, when Mor's head appeared over the fence, half hidden by swirling fog. The lava was no barrier to him either.

"Die, thief!" Mor bellowed.

Skarde grabbed the hilt of the sword with a gloved hand and leapt away. The giant's hammer came flying like a thunderbolt and crashed through the stalagmite fence like it was made of sticks. Skarde rolled away. Despite his mongoose-like speed, the hammer swung close, and a spray of rock shards cut Skarde's back. He dove down the passage to the cavern below, sliding painfully on his ass halfway. Pulling his hand away from the hot brand, it clattered down just ahead of him, knocking off some hardening rock that still clung to the blade. He picked it up again with his left hand and ran to exit the small side tunnel.

The giant had bombed across the span of the lava chamber and was already before him.

"I will crush you!" bellowed the giant. His eyes seemed to glow red with anger.

Mor swung his hammer and, too high, it crashed into the roof of the tunnel even as Skarde ducked low and past. Scree and dust tumbled down on Skarde. The giant spun and brought his hammer down, shattering the stone Skarde had just rolled away from.

"Give me the sword, mortal, for I shall deliver it to Gul-Zagar with or without your corpse!"

"To the Hells with you!" Skarde roared.

Switching the sword to his right hand again, as his left stung from heat, he flew on his long legs toward the trap. He reached the ground that Belgeti had warned him about and leapt for all he was worth. He came down near the far hole they had made, and it crumbled beneath his feet. His speed carried him and sent him sprawling on the floor. He rose and caught sight of the men thirty paces ahead. They looked back past him, horror on their faces. Skarde twisted as Mor careered on to the weakened floor and dropped with a howl. The impact shook the ground, the crash deafening.

A cloud of choking dust belched into the air. A petrichor scent filled the air, but his sight was blotted out in swirling darkness. Coughing, he stood, unsure where to strike. The rock powder rained down, and he could faintly see a feminine figure illuminated by the red glow. The lava behind her seemed to pulse forward.

"Sulmei!" Skarde called out.

"Strike now!" she screamed.

Skarde could barely make out the lip of the newly formed crater. He approached the edge, his eyes searching out for Mor. He caught a glimpse of two eyes like red-hot coals staring up at him in fury. Then, like a boulder cast from a mountaintop, the giant's hammer hurtled towards him. He scrambled back, and the hammer's face crashed into the rim of the stony cauldron. Slivers of sharp debris cut him, and his ears rang as he stumbled back. For a moment he lost his sense of balance and the world tumbled. He forced his dust clogged eyes open and saw that Mor had planted his torso sized hands on the lip of the hole and was lifting his massive frame upwards. Skarde scrambled back as the monster rose and stood before him.

Mor had escaped their trap.

Skarde bounded to his feet, glared up at the giant, and raised his sword. "Come, dog, and die!"

Mor laughed and took a stride forward. Skarde's eyes widened at the coming giant. From the red, swirling dust, a lithe figure flew. Sulmei, her dagger drawn, made a colossal leap over the cavity, and landed with hardly her toes alone at the crumbling edge. She sprang forward, and even as Mor raised his hammer to strike Skarde, she drove her blade into the giant's mid-calf from behind. Though the gleaming silver blade seemed like but a thorn against the brute, Mor let out a stone-shattering howl.

His senses took in the events of a moment at a manic pace as warriors do when death is only a hair's breadth away. Skarde moved like a striking snake. The bellowing giant, a look of agony on his face, tumbled over him even as he struck. Skarde dashed to the side, and narrowly dodged the giant's blow. He glanced at Sulmei, and his heart froze. She held the dagger, ready to strike again, and blood dripped from its edge. Her eyes glowed like hot coals; her teeth clenched; a look of fury was like a mask upon her face. She gazed murder at Skarde.

"Kill!" she thundered, her voice unnaturally deep and cavernous.

She needed not to command him. Never ceasing to move, he pounced up Mor's arm as he crashed to the ground, and then mounted his back. Skarde plunged the sword to the left of his spine, and the tip drove in with far more ease than he anticipated. The giant's hand reached back and curled about Skarde's leg as the sword bit deep. Mor howled an unholy howl, and Skarde was dragged down and crushed under the giant's left arm. Skarde tensed his corded muscles before his spine was broken or his guts crushed. He bellowed a curse in defiance as Mor glared at him. He saw in Mor's eyes disbelief and hate unbound as the pressure on Skarde mounted to an unbearable intensity. The mountain seemed to shake, and the staid air of the tunnel erupted in a sudden swirling tempest. Skarde shut his eyes as the raging winds drove biting hot gritted across his face. Mor let out a keening wail, and the wind suddenly ceased. Skarde dared a glance.

The fire and light in the giant's eyes dimmed, and he was no more.

"Thunir!" Skarde choked, almost inaudibly.

He pushed at the crook of Mor's elbow with all his might. He felt it shift, but his breath was leaving him. It was as if the father of all bears slumbered on his chest. Sulmei flew over his arm like a living storm, grabbed the giant's wrist, and hauled it upwards. Skarde stared at her dumbfounded.

"Move, mortal fool!" she roared with a voice as unnatural as her strength.

Skarde pushed at the arm for all he was worth and shuffled his legs. He broke free, and rolled out to lay against the dead giant's shoulder, gasping. Sulmei tossed the massive arm of the dead giant to the ground and stood as if a great weight rest upon her shoulders. Her naked body was coated in rock dust, and she looked like a statue of a figure carved in a moment of tragedy. Her eyes were clamped shut; her face contorted in some internal struggle.

"Sulmei," Skarde said. "Sulmei!" he now shouted.

She stood for a long moment, shook her head, and grunted. Her body quivered. "I will be Sulmei! I am Sulmei! I AM Sulmei!" she shouted, opening her mad eyes wide.

Her gaze turned on him, and she raised the dagger high.

"Sulmei!" Skarde shouted again. "Mor is dead!"

He gestured at the giant's face, right beside him. Sulmei turned and considered it, breathing heavy. He wondered at what madness had overcome her, and where she got the strength to lift the giant's arm.

"Put your dagger away," he said, eyeing it. He liked the look of it even less now.

She looked at it, and her eyes seemed to return to the here and now. She sheathed the dagger and stared at Skarde. Feeling recovered enough to stand and fearing Sulmei's hideous steel tongue, he rolled to his feet. He clambered upon the giant's back. He gripped the sword and pulled it out of its sheath of flesh. He held it high, and the blade quivered in his hand. The grip was again almost too hot to touch. Something, Skarde knew not what, was markedly different about the weapon.

The men howled in triumph, and he shook the sword above him in victory. At that moment, the whole cavern seemed to shake and rumble. Skarde looked back, and the edge of the lava lake he could see sputtered and surged forward. Skarde hopped down and took Sulmei by the shoulder.

"Let us go," Skarde moved, and she ran along with him. "Run!" he barked at the men, and they sped on ahead of him.

With but a single torch held by Kasuk they fled up the narrowing tunnel, and then crawled up the fissures that led to the roof of Grim-Face's work area. There, Kasuk tied off the rope his brother Farasid carried. They looked down and saw slaves chopping at the rocks but looking about unsure as the mountain trembled. Kasuk motioned to Sulmei.

"You first, lady. We shall lower you."

Sulmei nodded and took hold of a length of rope with steady hands. She slipped down into the cavity. Grim-Face's men all about gazed up in surprise as Sulmei descended gracefully, like a spider on a silk line among them.

Chapter Fifteen

Skarde and his companions stood in a semi circle as the last of them climbed down from the shadowed ceiling. Grim-Face watched them as if a troupe of acrobats had appeared in a village. Belgeti came last and landed lightly as a mighty cracking sound thundered through the mines. The men flinched and looked about wide-eyed.

"The spirit of the mountain is angry," Belgeti said. "You angered it by killing the giant, Skarde."

Grim-Face gazed at Skarde with a grave look. "I would hear this tale, but the rumbling is a worry. What madness does Belgeti speak of?"

"Belgeti speaks true," Skarde said. "The mountain is angered. Fire will come. We must escape the mines. We must escape the citadel!"

"I have prepared the men. Come!" Grim-Face shouted. "We must fight now or die!"

The men gripped their picks and let out a battle cry, though not all looked pleased.

Skarde gathered Grim-Face, Belgeti, Sulmei and Tarsazi. "Go to the gate hall, Grim-Face, and see if Wrinkles will open up for you. If he has any sense, he will. Sulmei and Tarsazi, go with him. I will join you soon. Belgeti, tell Peg-Leg. I will get my men."

Sulmei had an unearthly glint in her eye, but she like the others had no disagreements. They hurried on to their tasks. Belgeti and Skarde traveled together, and met several bullies and slaves alike confused in the tunnels. Skarde was near the main concourse when his men, having already abandoned their work, rushed out to meet them. Belgeti signaled his temporary parting and went on ahead to meet Peg-Leg and Skarde led his own to the gate.

"Our time is here," Skarde spoke aloud. "A fight we may have at the gate, and certainly trouble awaits us beyond. I crave a fight! Let's have no more of this toil and darkness!"

Jarrod, though he appeared withered, raised his pick and howled a war cry. His spirit soothed Skarde's doubts. The others cheered and shook their picks above their heads. Skarde led them on, and they joined with others fleeing alone or in small groups toward the only exit. As they hit the main concourse, a tremor struck, and nearly knocked several off their feet. A blistering crack echoed through the cavern and the floor split. Skarde leapt aside, as a jet of steam blasted upward. Men screamed in pain, and one fell dead. Abruptly the jet ceased, and the men surged forward, both fear and determination on their faces.

The gate room was a riot when Skarde arrived. Four of the less tractable bullies had taken up on the stairs to Absi's chancery. They wielded swords; no doubt supplied on the spot by Absi. The old taskmaster himself leered out of his barred window, bellowing for all to return.

"The Master will have your heads if you rebel!" Absi screamed above the din. "Return to work, fools! The mountain only grumbles!"

"Open the gate, Absi!" Skarde yelled back. "The mountain will burn us all alive!"

"You were always trouble," Absi said. "You and that witch! Do not be deceived! Return you all to the mines!"

"Nine Hells! You obstinate fool!" Skarde said, and he ran to the base of the stairs.

"Move," he said to Burned-Man.

"For the Brotherhood of Iron!" he called and brandished his sword.

Skarde grimaced. Burned-Man was a believer. He might have been convinced to cooperate in time but needs pressed. Skarde charged up the stairs and blocked a blow from Burned-Man's blade. The other swordsmen jostled for position, but the space was tight. Skarde thrust and they traded blows. His sword moved with weight and ease, as if it desired to bite into flesh. The metal rang, yet with a lower pitch and different timbre than steel. In a moment, Skarde won through and slashed his opponent's legs. Burned-Man toppled off the stairs and might have gotten up if he hadn't been set upon by a crowd of slaves hewing at him with their picks.

"Come down and join us!" Skarde barked at the three remaining swordsmen.

They glanced at each other and lowered their swords. Skarde backed up, holding his sword up, wary of sudden attack, as the three descended. Before Skarde could ascend the stairs to argue with Absi, a dozen men rushed up. They began hacking at the door. Two of the larger men, giants almost the size of Skarde pressed their way up and took their turn. In a minute, the sturdy door had been hacked off its stony moorings. They rushed inside. Absi's scream gurgled to silence moments later, and out came one of the big slaves holding a plain iron key over his head. The assembled slaves roared a cheer and parted a path for the man as he strode forth, a champion.

He unlocked the gate, and they poured out into the tunnels of the citadel with thunder and triumph. Skarde kept an eye on the three reluctant guards and moved along with Peg-Leg and Sulmei as the gate room emptied.

"That is an end to our sly departure," Skarde laughed.

Peg-Leg and Sulmei both glared at him with grim eyes.

"As if the trembling mountain will not stir up all the guard like a hive of wasps shaken!"

As if to lend him credence, the gate room thundered and cracked, filling with scalding steam. They ran along the passage upward when suddenly an uproar halted their progress.

Swordsmen of the brotherhood poured from a side passage, and weapons were drawn. Many of the slaves screamed and ran back, and Skarde pushed his way forward. Several slaves ahead of him were skewered on steel.

Skarde roared and slew a surprised swordsman. Three others surrounded him, and he battered their attacks away with a grim smile on his face. As he did, several brave slaves attacked the three from their flank, and in a grim fray, the three were slain, with as many slaves joining them. A stout armed, grey-haired slave tossed his pick aside, and gathered up the fallen soldier's swords.

"I can put this to good use," he said, swinging the brand in his hand. "And I know others skilled in sword fighting!"

"Good man!" Skarde answered.

They moved on. Some thirty of their men lay dead. and for the moment, unmourned. Many others were now equipped with swords and daggers. Skarde glanced behind as they ran and saw that Peg-Leg and Sulmei had fallen behind. Skarde retraced his steps, and just around the curving cavern, he saw Sulmei and Peg-Leg speaking. She kissed him gently and departed alone down yet another side tunnel. Skarde felt a twinge of jealousy. *Don't be a fool*, he thought to himself, *she is no man's. Yet perhaps it is not the kiss, but the confidence she bestows on him.* Peg-Leg jogged on towards him as fast as his leg would take him.

"Where does she go?" Skarde asked.

Peg-Leg shook his head. "She goes to Gul-Zagar's sanctum."

"Hodan's beard! That is madness!"

"You would not be deterred from bringing the whole of the slave work force, and she will not be deterred from whatever it is she seeks there."

"Should we not go with her?"

"No. She said we could not gain entrance to his sanctum, and even if we could, we would be of little help. Let us go on. She will find us," Peg-Leg said.

Skarde grumbled. His inclination was to disregard Peg-Leg and go after Sulmei. His sense of honor demanded it, but she was no ordinary woman, and the affairs of sorcerers were not his to meddle in. Shaking his head, he ran on with the escaped slaves. They made for the fighting pit. Beyond that lay the main gates.

When they neared the fighting pit, the sword tingled in his grasp. *Kill him*, Skarde thought he heard. *Kill him!* Looking about he saw it was not one of the men. Not even a voice to be heard by the ear. *Kill him! I feel it. He is in there!* He heard the words in his mind, but more unnerving, he could feel hate. A thirst for revenge. It wasn't his own. Or was it? He held up the sword.

"You thirst for blood?" Skarde said.

"Are you well?" Peg-Leg asked, stopping to look with concern at Skarde.

I will taste your blood too. Yet, I shall delay payment for your misdeeds, mortal, Skarde heard the voice faintly. Not as a whisper, but as a great voice far in the distance. *Spill the blood of the traitor and appease me. Kill Gul-Zagar!*

Skarde felt his feet move. Gul-Zagar was in the gladiatorum. He knew… or the sword knew. Skarde recalled his capture, his trials in the jungle, and his hardships in the mines.

"Yes… I will take revenge," Skarde said.

"Skarde! What are you talking about," Peg-Leg said.

Without a word, Skarde took long strides toward the pit. He passed under the great arches and felt a tingle down his spine. There, across darkened sand sat Gul-Zagar upon his throne, illuminated by two newly lit torches. He seemed lost in contemplation, motionless, and meditating. Skarde thought as he approached that he saw his face drawn long and disappointment in his furrowed brow. *More emotion than I have seen upon his face ever yet.*

"Have you come for revenge, warrior?" Gul-Zagar's voice filled the great dark chamber. "Or do I await revenge upon you?"

"I come for blood, wizard!" Skarde said, quickening his pace. "This you know."

Gul-Zagar stood and held out his hand. Skarde feared some spell, but he felt nothing supernatural.

"All this I built," Gul-Zagar said as the ground trembled. "And here upon this seat, I felt the bones of the mountain most keenly… and let my thoughts dwell upon my designs for the future where all could stand on stone, feel the sunlight, and fear not the night."

"Your designs, wizard, built on misery and chains!"

"What substance you give to such petty things." Gul-Zagar shook his head.

Kill him! I demand blood! Skarde heard in his mind.

"I see by that sword that you have betrayed me. I hear its call as you do and know that Sulmei has also betrayed me. For what? To satisfy your petty desires? To kill. To destroy. To steal a few baubles? To flee your burdens? These are the ambitions of children. What do these matter against the destiny I offered you? Glory eternal in a world made paradise. That is what I offered you. I hear the sword's demand. It is a vessel made not for the spirit that inhabits it. It is of no use to me now. But it will make use of you, Skarde. You wield it not. It is a blade that wields you, and you gladly succumb to it."

He stood.

"Go. Be free if you think that is what you will have. Return to your vagabond life, wandering blind in the lawless darkness, a thief, a murderer, mighty until your might fails, and you are trod into the earth by another wandering butcher. I waste words on you and have much to do. Begone."

Gul-Zagar pulled from his robes two round stones and held them up in his palm. He spoke a word, and the stones began to shine with an eerie light. He tossed them and they landed in the sand a few paces from Skarde's feet. The moment they landed, the sand rippled like water about the stones, and they sank. Skarde felt a deep rumble under his feet, and he backed away cautiously. Something arose from the ground, and sand poured off it like water down a mountain. Skarde saw the stones glowing now like two eyes. They were set in a stony rough-hewn face upon a block of a head. The shoulders of the creature were as big as an ox, and the arms that hung at its side were as thick as its brick-like torso. It stepped forward on short, powerful legs. It raised a fist and brought it down like a hammer.

Skarde hurled himself out of the way with a curse and ran. The stone brute plodded after him. He dared to look back as he passed through the arching corridor and into the tunnels. The weird stone brute only moved at a walking pace, but his heart was not set at ease. *I will run out of places to run, and then how might I fight stone with a sword?* He ran on toward the exit, hoping for some answer to present itself. *Perhaps they have broken the front gates and flee into the jungle even now!*

Skarde slowed as he neared the antechamber to the hall of the main gate room. There, Peg-Leg and Sulmei raced back toward him. Skarde wondered at Sulmei. She wore the head dress of silvered feathers and the accompanying regalia. They met and halted.

"Is *that* what you returned for?" Skarde said, eyeing the extravagance.

Sulmei, with a strange light still in her eye, nodded. "I returned for these most valuable tomes," she said holding up a leather satchel. "The regalia will do Gul-Zagar no good."

"Tyhomir is just ahead," Peg-Leg cut in. "The slaves have won through to the gate and fight for it, but the captain and his men will carve them up from behind. We must go!"

"And be hasty! Gul-Zagar has summoned a thing of stone to see us off. We may not return down this tunnel," Skarde said. Already its heavy footstep could be heard echoing.

"An earth elemental!" Sulmei said. "We can not battle it. It will crush us. Let's go!"

They rushed into the expansive ante-chamber, and Skarde grumbled under his breath. There, Tyhomir and his men awaited him. The open space gave the Iron Brotherhood the advantage. Twenty swordsmen stood with him. In the tunnels, Skarde might have fought one or two at a time. Even then, he would be cut down in time, but here he could be surrounded and hacked to pieces. He glanced about. The elemental could be heard behind them. There were other tunnels, but none led out. Either Gul-Zagar's summoned spirit, or the rumbling mountain would kill them.

"I knew the Master could not trust you, she-dog. You've led these two about by the nose. This revolt is your doing. Once dead, I will put things right again!" Tyhomir said.

Skarde breathed deep. "Valhalla, I come!" He stepped forward, swinging his sword. "The slave revolt is my doing. Come and die!"

It was empty bluster and Tyhomir laughed. "Toran was right to put you in the mines. I will bury you there. Men! Attack!"

The men called out an "Aye!" and spread out as they approached him. Skarde heard a growl. Sulmei brushed past him and stood between him and his opponents with clenched fists.

"Sulmei!" Skarde called out.

She let out a keening wail, and a shiver of terror ran down his spine. She held forth her hands, her fingers spread wide, and flames licked at her body. The faint glowing tongues roared suddenly about her. Tyhomir looked wide-eyed and threw himself to the ground. The men rushed her, but a blast of fire blazed out in a fan from her outstretched hands. Skarde and Peg-Leg both grimaced and covered their faces at the dreadful heat. The swordsmen, caught in the flames, screamed in agony. Their armor charred, and their flesh melted from their faces.

Skarde could hardly breathe the scorching air as their enemy's bodies clattered to the floor. Peg-Leg gasped. Nearly blinded by the flash, Skarde peered out from behind his guarding hand. The scene came into view as his vision returned, and he looked on in horror. He did not see Tyhomir's body among them. The smoking corpses let off a nauseating sweet and putrid stench. Sulmei stood, now seemingly calm, amid the swirling death-smoke.

"Hodan!" Skarde swore. "Let us go, quickly!" he added, hearing the elemental's thudding footsteps grow loud behind them.

They dashed forward, and as they neared the front gate, Skarde heard the din of battle over their footfalls and huffing. He took no time for caution and dove into the bailey. A terrible melee sprawled across the whole cavern. A hundred sword and bow men battled three times as many slaves. Screams echoed from the walls and blood spilled. Upon the steps to the winch-room over the portcullis stood Belgeti and another slave. Belgeti held up a stolen bow and knocked an arrow. It seemed to Skarde that the weight of age upon Belgeti was sloughed off as he drew the arrow back. His back straightened and his eyes caught his target like an eagle. The arrow flew across the court and an enemy bowman dropped to the ground with a cry.

Skarde roared and swung his sword, marveling at the ease with which he delivered heavy blows and sharp cuts. The feel of a sword in his hand stirred his heart too, and he pressed his way on toward Belgeti. Outside the portcullis a dull light came, and Skarde scented a storm in the air. His lungs ached for a taste. Three swordsmen he laid low, his sword singing, and others gave way before him. Belgeti and his companion had gone into the winch-room, and now came back out. Catching sight of Skarde, he waved his bow over his head.

"The crazy guard has cut the ropes! It will take some work to fix!" Belgeti shouted over the noise.

Skarde turned toward Sulmei. Peg-Leg stood near her, his sword up defensively, though none approached the sorceress. They caught his gaze. "The gate is broken!" he yelled, gesturing at the portcullis, and shaking his head.

"Ho! Stop fighting, all! This is madness!" Skarde bellowed over the melee.

His deep voice was lost in a sea of manly timbres. Sulmei grimaced and stood forward. She raised up her hands to her mouth and inhaled deeply.

"Aiiiiiiii!" She wailed, a piercing note.

Skarde took a step back, his instincts warning of danger. He imagined she might again send a murderous fan of flames from her outstretched arms. She spoke and her voice filled the chamber, not unlike Gul-Zagar's voice had boomed, though womanly.

"The spirit of the mountain is angered! The volcano will send fire and death! Cease your fighting – open the gate or die!"

Her proclamation was followed by a shudder, and rock crumbled in scree from the ceiling. There was a flash of red through the portcullis and the hiss of steam like a sword plunged into water.

Skarde strode toward the iron lattice. "To me!" he cried, pointing at a handful of the burliest slaves. Swords held in mid swing lowered guardedly and five big men joined him before the gate. They dropped their weapons, squatted low, and gripped the thick cold iron bar.

"With me now!"

They grunted. Corded muscles bulged against the mighty weight and still it held to the ground. Sulmei came running, and behind her, the clatter of stony feet on a stony floor rumbled. The men stood and regained their breath as they looked toward the far tunnel entrance for the source of the strange noise. Skarde and the others caught a grim look in Sulmei's eyes.

"The elemental comes!" Sulmei cried.

Teeth clenched, she dropped to her haunches beside Skarde, and gripped the iron. Skarde's eyes widened. She was an athletic woman, to be sure, but dwarfed by the men. Skarde again grabbed the bar with her, and the others followed his lead. Their muscles bulged once more, but this time the portcullis lifted with a scrape. They had lifted it a few feet when Skarde heard a ruckus behind him. He turned his head. The elemental had emerged from the tunnel and men scrambled out of its path. It came straight for him.

"It's after me! I have a plan!" Skarde bellowed.

He let go of the iron, kicked his sword underneath, and rolled under the teeth of the massive gate.

"Let go!" He said, picking up his weapon. "Back away!"

All let go. Sulmei held on last, her arms quivering to support the massive iron portcullis. *How does she summon such titanic strength?* He wondered not long, as the glowing eyes of the elemental fixed upon him.

"Come, demon! I am here!" he taunted the monster, swinging his sword.

The men dodged out of the gateway, and Sulmei rolled gracefully, managing even to keep her diadem of long silver feathers in place. The heavy iron bars crashed to the stone floor with a terrific clang. The elemental charged the gate, and a great fist flew like a bolt at the portcullis. It rang like thunder and shook in its moorings. Dust and stone chips flew down over him. The creature pounded on the grill, and it bent toward him. Skarde, his spine tingling, backed away as the lower right corner clattered up and scraped over stone. Another hit, and the lower edge came free. It occurred to Skarde that the elemental was vastly strong and could have just lifted the portcullis, but now it stepped forward and bent the whole thing toward the roof.

"Thunir's axe!" Skarde swore.

He ran. A glowing patch of light grew ahead of him. Like a bat from the bowels of the earth he emerged from the wide-mouthed tunnel. The grim, iron-grey sky stung his eyes like dazzling sunshine. Cool rain washed the dry caked dust from his flesh. Down the mountainside ran long creeping fingers of glowing orange lava, and billowing clouds of hissing steam spurted skyward. He laughed in triumph and mirth even as the brutal conjuration followed close on his heel.

Chapter Sixteen

Skarde raced down the jungle path, the free air in his lungs. The thundering earth elemental plodded on behind him, but he soon put it happily out of sight. He stopped for a moment to stare, eyes a-wonder, at the spectacle the mountain was displaying. Tendrils of molten rock covered its face like red veins. Suddenly, rock exploded from its uppermost heights and sent glowing embers flying high through the sky. A moment later, a bang like no thunder he had ever before heard ripped the air.

"Luwydi, what a madness this is to see!" he said.

He stood for a long moment, eyes unblinking at the beauty and might of the erupting volcano. He wondered what force or what spirit could cause such destruction? What else it might be capable of? What other secrets lay under the earth? His ears caught the faintest crashing footstep in the distance over the din of the fire and storm. He turned and sprinted on lest the elemental find him again, when hot debris pelted him from behind, singeing his skin. Red hot grit, none larger than a pebble assailed him. He roared at the pain and glanced back. Clouds of rolling ash hurtled like spears down the mountain, and rents cracked the solid stone sending up ominous red glows.

Abruptly, a terrific crack blasted the air and the ground shuddered. The stony path ahead split and flaming red death vomited forth. Skarde scrambled to a halt sending a spray of wet sand and pebbles sizzling into the belching lava. He dashed to outpace the growing wound in the earth, and one around it he ran reckless through the jungle back toward the path. Here the earth sank, and a jet of boiling vapors jetted into the air. There, another crack rent the earth, and spewed magma.

His tireless pace put him ahead of immediate danger, he guessed, and he turned his mind to how he might join up with his companions and complete their plan to escape the island. He hid among the trees. He could not trust the swordsmen, even if they had made a temporary peace to struggle with the portcullis. *What of Sulmei? She is a greater mystery now than ever,* he thought. He wondered at her strange behavior after she had stabbed Mor, and her newfound gigantic strength. *Curse sorcery. It's a strange thing.*

Down the trail came groups of slaves and swordsmen alike. He clenched the bare metal grip of his new sword, ready for trouble. Then, a whistling comet of blazing red light hurtled down and exploded just off the path between them.

"Hodan!" Skarde swore. They were not safe from the mountain yet.

The slaves and swordsmen flinched at the blast and the roaring fire it produced. For the moment, both groups appeared to be more interested in escaping the vengeful mountain than in fighting each other. They picked each other up and ran on. *How long will a truce last?*

He caught sight of Sulmei, a striking figure among the beleaguered mobs. Her ostentatious ornaments and crown of silver feathers caught the red glint of the fury of the mountain. The dust had been sluiced from her skin, as it had been from his, by the rain. Unclothed, her head held high, she looked all the more out of place in the rout. Peg-Leg hobbled on beside her, his sword out and his gait self-assured despite his debility. Skarde rushed out of the trees and up the path to meet them.

"Ho!" Skarde called, seeing them. "You live! I am glad to see it."

"Your deed was madness!" Peg-Leg barked.

"Yet it worked," Sulmei said, putting a hand on his shoulder.

Peg-Leg's face softened. "Aye, I suppose it did. But only just."

Skarde glanced back up the trail, though not far off trees blocked his vision. "Where might that gargantuan stone monster be?"

"Lucky for you, it has turned back to the citadel," Sulmei said. "It scattered hundreds of fleeing men off the trail as it went. Do not let down your guard. It may be that it has just lost your trail and returns to its master for instruction."

"Let down my guard!" Skarde laughed. "We have only an army of swordsmen about us who may be rallied against us at any moment, and a ship to commandeer. Aye, I thought to put myself at ease."

"Well, to both those points – make haste!" Sulmei said.

"Lead on. Where shall we go? I do not know the way to these new docks you spoke of."

"Onward, at the very least to outpace the anger of the volcano," she said. "Then before the beaches, we take a newly cut path on the right. There we will circle about the island to its western side."

They continued, though Skarde kept looking back, not for the elemental, but for his men. He was gladdened to catch sight of Belgeti. He bid Sulmei and Peg-Leg to move on, and he ran back. He moved back along the line of fleeing men. They greeted each other, grabbing each other's forearms.

"So, the wizard's pet didn't crush you. Too hard a nut?"

"Too fast a dog, more like. It is good to see you," Skarde said.

"Where do we go now?" Belgeti asked.

Skarde explained where the docks lay. "We will stop and meet on the trail further on, or in the village, for it lays that way. Run back and gather all the once-slaves who would fight and sail for freedom. Lead them forth and we shall rush the docks, whatever we find there."

Belgeti nodded and sped back. Skarde ran forward and found Sulmei and Peg-Leg just before they turned on to the westward jungle path. Lightning flashed above them, and choking hot ash poured from the sky. Skarde ducked low and the rest followed his lead as the sky darkened. Ahead, they heard a tremendous impact, and fires sprang up blocking their path despite the heavy rain.

"The volcano flings fiery rocks at us. Is there nothing you can do, Sulmei, to appease it, or lessen its strength?"

"I have power over fire, yes, but that is beyond me," she said.

They clambered through the uncleared jungle, avoiding the burning path, and soon found themselves back on the trail.

"What other powers do you possess?" Skarde said when they had sorted themselves. "You lifted the giant's arm when I could not, and without you, we would not have raised the portcullis. You must have the strength of ten men!"

"I don't know. Only that now I feel a great strength in my limbs," Sulmei said. She did not meet his gaze.

"I saw a light shine in your eye when you stabbed Mor's calf. Is that it?"

Sulmei said nothing and walked on, her eyes focused on the rough road ahead of them.

"Aye, it is. Just as my sword has drunk in Mor's spirit, so your dagger took something from him..."

Sulmei turned and gave him a stern look. "It is a dangerous and evil thing you ask about. Would you learn sorcery, too? Ask me no more!"

Skarde opened his mouth to argue, but he held back. *Kill her! She conspired all along! Betrayer!* Some voice whispered in his mind. Skarde shook his head. *Silence!* He answered back. He gave his sword a troubled glance, and he pushed the thought far away.

"Dangerous and evil," he muttered to himself.

They trudged along for hours. More men caught up with them, and Skarde kept them moving briskly. Though he dreaded not the elemental for the moment, he grew concerned that if the docks were too well defended, their plans would be dashed. Then, as they rounded a hillock that stood under an outstretched arm of the mountain, he came across a familiar village. The same village whose inhabitants had aided him.

He slowed his pace and looked over a scene of devastation. A chill hand gripped his stomach. Ash was strewn over the fields. Some huts burned, while others were blackened and half collapsed. In an open space, Skarde saw the occasional searing red comet pelt down. He saw bodies, hither and thither. Certainly, many had escaped, but not all. Sulmei and Peg-Leg drew him on with soothing words. He ran to a body and examined it; his jaw clenched. He couldn't make out who it was – the elder who had aided him or another. It didn't matter. A shadow passed over his heart.

"I would have repaid the old man named Pyae, and the village if I could. Instead, I brought them ruin," Skarde said in a melancholy tone.

"This is not your doing," Peg-Leg said. "Come, see... some slaves already follow behind us. Let us..."

Skarde ignored him and rushed off toward a sobbing sound. In a partly collapsed hut squatted a white-haired old woman. She made a mewling sound in between wails. He bent down to look at her. She seemed unhurt, but stared into the distance unblinking, ignoring his approach.

"Ho, grandmother," Skarde said. "Are you hurt?"

She wailed as if she saw something, though her eyes neither blinked nor moved. Skarde doubted she could understand him, at least fully, but he spoke in a kindly timbre.

"Have the others escaped? Are they well?"

She said nothing other than sad incomprehensible murmurs. Skarde sensed Sulmei at his side.

"I'm sorry," Sulmei said. "There is nothing we can do for her now. We cannot tarry without risking a confrontation with the loyal soldiers of the Iron Brotherhood."

"Belgeti is here," Peg-Leg said. "Almost three hundred slaves follow close behind."

Skarde turned and looked out where the old woman stared.

"Skarde," Belgeti said.

Skarde seemed not to hear. Turning to Peg-Leg he shook his head. "The sight is awful and has rattled him."

"Skarde!" Peg-Leg said. "Will you lead the slaves, or I?"

Skarde turned and saw that Jarrod had joined them.

"Me and Belgeti spoke with the men," Jarrod said. "Not all will fight to board a ship. Some are too old, or not apt in battle. I am of like mind. We will stay. Many villagers have fled, Skarde. Some will return. We will stay and rebuild. A hut and a field are a paradise compared to the mines. We will leave when safe passage avails itself... or stay. Who knows?"

"Are you sure that is wise?" Skarde said.

Jarrod sat on the ground near the stricken old woman. "Who knows what path is wise? None are safe. I will watch over her for a while. She may know where survivors have gone. The citadel of Gul-Zagar is destroyed. He will leave, and so will the Brotherhood."

"Gul-Zagar is, I expect, already gone," Sulmei said. "His sanctum is not entirely of this earth. When he closes its door, he may open it somewhere else."

"I'm not sure what it is you say," Belgeti said.

"I cannot expound further now. Just know he is gone. He would not tarry here over vexation and regret," Sulmei said. "No doubt, he is already planning anew."

Skarde nodded, soberly. "Time for regret later."

"Aye," Belgeti said holding up his newfound bow. "Maybe a hundred of us will fight. Fierce men all."

Blood pumped again through Skarde's frozen heart. "Lead on Sulmei."

Skarde moved slowly toward the forest edge with Sulmei. Peg-Leg tarried, awaiting Belgeti and his men. The freed slaves gripped each other by the arm and said their farewells. Skarde caught snippets of oaths, well wishes, and hopes for brighter times. The parting took more time than Skarde thought safe. He stood still, facing the dusky foliage still, not like a tree, but as a hunting cat eager to pounce. He listened for any sound of approaching swordsmen. His stomach tightening and his tolerance at an end, he paced back and forth.

"Those that know each other in dark times often make fast friends," Sulmei said. "Be patient."

"Aye, but we have need of haste!"

Sulmei eyed him knowingly.

"Also, the ruined village is a grim thing to dawdle near," he added.

Skarde's hand squeezed the bare metal grip of the sword impatiently, yet he held back a shout. It was Belgeti that turned his face to the sky and let out a far-reaching rallying cry in the fashion of his people. A hundred pairs of eyes turned to him, and he cried out again and waved his bow in the air. Holding it high as if he would shoot an arrow into the grey clouds overhead, he marched along the trail, and others followed him.

Skarde smiled, and his heart beat hard to move on. "I am glad of Belgeti," he said to Sulmei. "His tales of war were not just boasts. He leads the men like a captain."

"There are other warriors among them," Sulmei said. "And others who will learn quick enough."

Skarde smiled. "And what about you? With your newfound strength you would make a deadly warrior. Would you take up a sword?"

Sulmei laughed. "Will the strength last? Even if it does, I would not take well to being skewered. I'll gladly leave that to others. I am no warrior."

"You leapt over a chasm and drove steel into a giant's leg. You are more a warrior than you think."

"An act of desperation," Sulmei said. "It was fear of having that sword you hold being driven into my chest that drove me to fight."

"Aye. That's often how it begins."

Chapter Seventeen

The men crossed the fields and now gathered around Skarde, Peg-Leg, and Sulmei. They formed a loose column, which suited him well enough. There was no time for drilling or formation. He lifted his sword and cried out an order to follow. A flaming rock sizzled high through the air. The volcano's fingers were stretching ever further out, but rather than frightening the men, it lit a fire in their spirits. They marched swiftly, and soon rounded a headland. Following a path downward they soon spotted the docks on the beach below.

Skarde nodded in approval when he could finally make it out clear through the rain and swirling mists. Even from afar, he could see it was solidly built. A dockmaster's house was there built of stone, as sturdy as a small castle. Not far off lay a sawmill with a great waterwheel that dipped into a short waterfall from a stream coming off the headland. Just a little further on was a long wooden pier and from it, four docks spread out. Upon one was a vessel half built and held up by timbers, and further out was a new, fine-looking ship. A long clinker-built, it had two furled sails upon great masts, and a single row of oars, held high out of the water like wings. There were thirty or so men arrayed on the grounds between the dockmaster's house and the docks. They spotted the slave army just as Skarde got their count. Belgeti ran to Skarde's side.

"About a score of us have bows. Say I run down ahead of you, and we give them a few volleys before you charge?"

"Aye, good! Run quick and soften them up," Skarde said.

Belgeti and a rag tag crew of bowman ran down the hill. The soldiers near the docks hesitated, seeing a smaller group break off, but soon retreated to the ship. Skarde cupped his hands to his mouth and cried out like Belgeti had done earlier.

"Now is the time, men!" he shouted. "They will lift the gangplank on us before we get up. You – Tarsazi, Farasid, and Kasuk! Follow me. We will try the saw house and find some timbers we can throw to climb up. Come now all! Fight and be free!"

Skarde let out a roar and held his sword to the lightning blasted sky. The men cried back with a fury and followed hot on his heels as he ran down the last of the road. Belgeti had already taken up position a hundred or so paces ahead when Skarde and the others reached the sawmill. He and the three others saw there was a plentiful selection of raw and cleaned trunks. Skarde quickly chose one about twenty feet in length, and the others chose alike. He slung it over his shoulder and ran at a surprising pace with the awkward weight. A flight of arrows whistled through the air into the ship. *Has Belgeti slain anyone? At least their own archers do not shoot back,* Skarde thought.

The boards of the pier rumbled and clattered as he raced along them, rising to a thunder as dozens followed him. The battle cry went up as Farasid threw down the first of the makeshift gang planks. The others did the same. Skarde tossed his down last as he took the far front of the ship. He flew up the trunk even before it stopped shaking and sprang up. A quick glance to his side revealed that Farasid and several other were tossed into the swelling sea by the ship's defenders. Kasuk topped the gunwale only to shriek and fall as an arrow sprung out of his chest. Tarsazi flung himself aside as an arrow narrowly skinned him, and others clambered up right after him. Skarde reached the top and threw himself over the gunwale and roughly on to the deck. He heard, but did not see, an arrow cut the air right above him.

Right away a small host of men, swords eager for death, rushed at him. He jumped to his feet, quick as a tiger, and slashed at a blade aimed at his head. He would have been stabbed through the side had it not been for his men flying on to the deck one after the other. Skarde roared and slashed as he pressed his enemy back. Again, he marveled at the smooth swing of his new blade. He turned and reversed it with ease, and a strike on his foe nearly split a leather cuirass in half.

Swords clashed and men screamed, in rage and in agony, as blood painted the decks. Skarde slew several. The number of corsairs aboard the ship almost matched the boarders. *These trained soldiers will overcome us*, Skarde thought. He fought on all the harder, but the freed slaves fought like demons. Their eyes burned with hate, their teeth clenched in snarls, as they lashed out with months of pent-up rage for their mistreatment. Their fury astonished Skarde. Even when one was impaled, he seemed to fight on, more intent on exacting revenge upon his former captors than defending himself. Skarde swung mighty blow after mighty blow. Blood flowed and bones cracked. Skarde raised his eyebrows, astounded when he found no foe to fight right before him.

A score of the corsairs retreated to the port side and flung themselves over the side to try their chances with the gnashing ocean. Three ex-slaves leapt over the side after them screaming for blood, and a few others had to be restrained. Skarde scanned the deck of the ship and saw they had won it. A raucous cheer went up.

"For captain Skarde, giant-slayer!" Several men roared, the same who had been with him in the tunnels beneath the mines.

Skarde smiled and thrust his sword high. *Captain. Aye, that has a good sound to it!*

"Check the lower decks!" Skarde bellowed over the din.

He and a few others rushed below, but no more of the Brotherhood of Iron was found lurking in the bowels of the vessel. Skarde returned to the top deck and another cheer went up. He looked across to the beach. Those few rag-tag escapees who hadn't drowned were pulling themselves from the crashing breakers. Belgeti and his archers took a few shots at them, but behind them, from around the headland, came a small army of soldiers.

Men shouted warnings but Belgeti was as sharp eyed as they. He and his fellows came pelting across the beach and along the pier. Belgeti ran up a makeshift plank, nimble as an old Billy goat, and the rest followed.

"Push off!" Skarde hollered.

He worked feverishly to launch the ship. There were a few among them who displayed their experience as sea-men, and under their guidance they were soon moving. Skarde was glad to see that some men who had fallen overboard had climbed back during the battle. Farasid was among them. He worked to push the ship away from the dock, his face a mask of sorrow. He had no doubt learned of his brother's demise.

They had hardly wafted five paces from the dock when some hundred soldiers charged across it only to stand there at the end feckless. Five paces may as well have been five miles. A few had bows, but their leader gave no order to fire. They were in no defensible position, unlike the new crew of the ship, and bow fire would go badly for them.

Skarde strutted to the rear starboard castle and gazed out over them. It was Toran himself who led the company. He gazed at Skarde with wrath. Skarde smiled back and raised his hand in salute. As his foe faded into the mist and rain, Skarde beheld the majesty and dread of the flame drenched mountain. *What power lies in the roots of the world!* He wondered. The din and bustle behind him reminded him that work needed doing.

Men ran to and fro, and much of the work was directed by a man once under Grim-Face's watch. Now he and others were raising a sail. Skarde, having some experience, wondered at this. Skarde spoke to him. Savo was his name, and he claimed experience as a sailor.

"Is it not foolhardy to raise a sail in such a storm?" Skarde asked.

"Aye, it is dangerous. But this fine ship has a storm sail. See, it is smaller and hardy. And I fear there may be other ships of The Master's fleet about. All speed is needed!"

"Very well, I shall help you raise it."

Then he and the others pulled ropes and heaved the sail into position against the potent grip of the wind. His hands still burning from the task, he saw that Tarsazi was organizing all that he could muster to descend to the lower deck and row. Skarde leapt up on the rope rigging by the main mast and bellowed a command for all who could to row. He marshalled two dozen men and with Tarsazi organized the task. Soon, some fifty oars were manned. Skarde climbed to the top deck and saw they were moving at a respectable speed.

Now, grimmer work was done on the top deck. Belgeti and a few others were tending to their wounded. Some of the men had taken to tossing the corpses of their foe over the side. Skarde halted their work.

"Let us bury them with respect," Skarde said.

"Would you perform some rite over them, Captain?" Grim-Face asked him.

"Nay. I have nothing to say. Most are of your race or near to it. Would you say some prayer to each as we give them to Ruen, goddess of the sea?"

"Tolos is our sea-god. He is grim and unknowable, but I will say a word in my tongue for each," Grim face said.

They sent ten of the Iron Brotherhood to the depths first, each body tumbling down and disappearing with haste in the dark tumult below them. Nine of their own they sent after, with more care. Friends for each came for a last farewell, but rain washed away all tears, and need shortened their mourning.

There was ever work to do as water filled the deck, ropes needed tightening, sails needed adjusting, and rowers given instruction. Skarde asked Savo to take the tiller. From the aft, Skarde looked back. The glow of the volcano was still seen through the storm, and his mind wandered across the strange places his feet had taken him over the past months. *A dream. Is it real? A tale for skalds and sorcerers.*

"Where is Sulmei," he wondered aloud.

Savo, beside him shrugged. Skarde's eyes swept the decks. She had stayed center deck and unmoving as the men jostled about her, with an otherworldly appearance. She was impossible to miss. Skarde ran below decks, and asked for her, but she wasn't there either.

"By the Nine Hells," Skarde said, returning to the top deck. "The mad witch!" He cried, looking up.

She had climbed the rigging and was now riding the wild raven's nest as the ship rocked in the rough sea. He called to her, but she did not answer back over the howling storm. Skarde felt the hilt of his sword tingle. *Kill her*, he heard a weighty whisper. In disgust, he thrust the tip into the deck and climbed the rigging. Her long silver feathers gamboled wildly in the wind, and glinted brightly as lightning flashed all too near. She held her arms high in supplication to the tempestuous rolling clouds as rain slashed at her naked body. He sprung off the rope rigging into the basket. Despite his sudden appearance, she kept her eyes closed, her face upturned and blissful.

"Do you summon or control the wind and lightning now with your sorcery, or be you mad?" Skarde said.

"Mad if you call it so. I do not control it. I exult in the might of the storm!"

As if called by her flattery, lightning slashed the sky too close and thunder ripped the air.

"Do you not feel it – coursing through your veins?" She said.

"I feel it," he said.

She turned to him, and stretching her body, she grabbed his neck and drew him forward to her lips. He kissed her as she clasped at his body.

"Take me now and crush me in your arms! Give your passion."

With a pounding heart and lightning in his veins, he took her, and their ardor roused them, untamed in the lashing storm. Delighting in victory and vitality even – nay moreso – under threat of flashing death.

The crew rowed all day and all night, and Skarde took his place on the oars and on the deck laboring as much as any other man. The storm receded into the south. At dawn, he shook the weight of a sleepless night off his limbs and the Sun cleared his tired eyes. He could spot no sail on the horizon, and his heart gladdened. Few had slept, so right away he called a *Thing* to speak with the leaders of the men. To Skarde came Peg-Leg, Sulmei, Belgeti, Grim-Face, Tarsazi, Savo, and others. As they spoke of the state of the ship and their hopes and thoughts, other men ceased their labors and gathered around to listen. Courtiers and councillors of civilized lands might have turned them away. Among Skarde's people, all who came had leave to listen and speak their part if they would, so he spoke aloud that all might hear him.

"You have fought for freedom and won through!" Skarde said. "Some have taken hurt, and some have died, and I honor you greatly. When tales are told of great deeds by campfires and by hearths, I will speak your names and say you fought like heroes and devils!"

A cheer went up, and Savo stood forth.

"Is it true you slew a giant in the heart of the mountain?" He said.

"Aye," said Sulmei. Tarsazi, Farasid, and Belgeti all echoed her in turn.

Skarde eyed the sword that now hung at his side in a belt rough made from rope. He said nothing of it.

"We must plot our course," Peg-Leg said.

"Aye," Skarde said. "I mean to take this fine ship pirating! We shall find fat merchant vessels foolish enough to sail without a small army aboard, and their booty will fill our hull to bursting."

Another cheer went up.

"For those with other desires, I will oblige to take you to whatever port might be practical for us, for you have won the ship and are free."

"I will follow!" Shouted several. "I too will sail with you!" said others.

Belgeti laughed. "My legs are made for the saddle, but what is a ship but a wooden horse upon hills of blue? I will try my luck pirating."

Skarde smiled.

"I will not go," Sulmei said. "My path leads elsewhere, far away."

"And I will follow you, Sulmei," Peg-Leg said.

Skarde nodded, rueful.

"We won't go far," Savo said, "without tightening our belts. We are low on provender. The ship was not ready to sail."

"Then let us head north. The league-ports of Byzerdamen there dot the coast," Skarde said.

"Those might be dangerous for the likes of us," said Savo. "We look like pirates at least, and suspicion will fall heavy on us. Further, we do not know what influence or allies Gul-Zagar had there."

"Aye," said Skarde. "Whether they love him or hate him, trouble would come of it. Is not the city of Goeška nestled there northward?"

"A thorn to Byzerdamen, and a lawless city," Peg-Leg said.

"Perfect," Skarde said. "There we sail!"

"And with what will we buy provisions?" asked Grim-Face.

Skarde pulled a purse that was tucked into his breeches. He opened it and pulled out a handful of rough but colorful stones.

"Gems, of course. I set them aside for myself, during my service to Gul-Zagar. They would keep me a few years in comfort I think, still more if I had them cut. Now, they will serve as coin for our sup."

Belgeti grinned wide. "You would make a passable horse-lord, young though you be."

Skarde grinned wide. Belgeti's confidence was not a thing he would lightly put aside. Skarde listened on as they spoke. The details bored him, and a problem pressed at his mind. He strode away from the group and stood upon the forecastle. Bow waves broke white against the hull splitting the blue-black depths, a little less fiercely now as most of the rowers had come up to listen to the plans being laid. *The wide ocean. The kingdom of Ruen is wide and perilous*, he thought. He felt anger, almost like a heat, radiating from the sword that now hung on his side. He drew it forth and his eyes swept along its strange grey metal. He sighed and held it over the rails. *Begone*, he thought, but his fingers hesitated.

"You won't be rid of its curse so easily," said a sympathetic feminine voice.

"Yet I would be rid of it. Gul-Zagar mocked me, saying the blade will wield me. It hates us and would see you dead. I felt his grip on my mind like his hand about my body. What use is a sword like that?"

Sulmei's fingertips slid along his outstretched arm and over his hand. "If you dropped it, it would reach out to the mind of some passing sea-creature and be dragged back to shore. There, it would be a magnificent find for someone... someone with less fortitude than you. You resisted Gul-Zagar's voice – no small feat. So long as you keep the sword, you keep it in your power. Ahh!"

Sulmei had slipped her fingertips over the naked blade. As her finger just touched the edge, blood dripped to the hungry sea below. Skarde felt a sudden murderous thrill. *The sword's bloodlust*, he knew.

"It is wickedly sharp!" She said.

"Despite the hard use I put it to yesterday, it suffered no notch or blemish," Skarde said.

"I thought so," Sulmei said licking the red trickle from her fingers, "that these swords would be near impossible to harm or destroy. I suspect it will never need sharpening. You could not dent it, even in a blacksmith's forge. I guess that I would need to summon a great heat from the depths of the earth in such a place as we had left behind, and some being like a giant to unmake it."

"A fine sword, but a curse," he said.

"Name it, at least. You may find some power over it in doing so."

"I name it Morsfangsel – Mor's prison. This I name both the sword and the metal." He carefully thrust the blade back into his belt.

"And what of you? Where do you go?" Skarde said.

"Come," she said.

Skarde and Sulmei went together to the captain's cabin, which Skarde had given to her so long as she stayed. Eyes followed them and some wore salacious grins. There, Sulmei took a moment to wrap a cloth around her bloodied fingers. She took up the satchel she had brought from the citadel and pulled from it a book.

Reclining on her bed she caressed its dark, plain leather bound cover. "A more ancient tome you will never see, Skarde. It has the same provenance as Gul-Zagar and was confined in a timeless prison with him for uncounted ages 'til locks made of star-stuff themselves unwound."

Skarde sat on the bed next to her. "I can read some letters, but I am no philosopher."

"You cannot read these letters. The script died with its people an eon ago. Still, look..."

She opened the book and found a spread with a map circle, and he gazed at it curiously.

"These are not maps of lands, but of stars and constellations," he said. "I have never seen the like."

"No. Do you recognize any?"

Skarde scanned the pages and felt a strange knot in his stomach, though he knew not why. "Is that the Hero's Chariot? And that near the horizon, is that the Longship?"

"I know not the names of the constellations in your land, and the stars in the South whence I come are different. Yet these stars are not the stars of our *time*, Skarde."

Skarde looked at her, unsure of her point.

"These are maps of places upon the earth, told by where the stars in the sky are. A convolution to dissuade the uninitiated from finding them. I wish to find these places, but I cannot find them as these stars are not our stars, but the stars of ages past. They move, Skarde. The stars move!"

Skarde wondered for a while. He shook his head "How? I would never have thought this. No doubt some priests would call that a heresy."

"Let them. I seek those who know more of this than I do. I seek now the Vuedethy priests of Angun. They have learned philosophers and astromancers. Perhaps, they can help me untangle these stars, and so find the places of a vanished civilization hidden by the deep mists of time."

Skarde's eyes widened as she spoke. He sighed deep and reclined on to the bed, resting his head on her lap. "What an extravagant plan. And I will sail, and fight and plunder," he said with melancholy.

"What is wrong, my love?"

"To me, it seems like you speak of chimera and the visions of prophets as things you may hold in your hands. The ways of wizardry are beyond me, and I rue it not. Yet... Gul-Zagar said that I was like a willful child who turns from a higher duty for a little prize. He spoke of a new world and a great glory that I spurned to fulfill my baser wants."

"A great glory for whom?" Sulmei asked. "I was to be forever enslaved in a blade. And were you to dig in a hole 'til your death. Should he choose our fate, and the fate of the whole world?"

Skarde turned suddenly and leapt over top of her. She laughed and he smiled. "I will love and laugh. I will fight and ride the four winds as is my heart's wont. That is the fate I make for myself. Maybe the philosophers you speak to can tell you who is right and who is wrong. It seems to me Gul-Zagar's 'greater purpose' was his own desire, and if he believed that he served it or merely said so to convince others means naught. Tyrants and priests are oft alike. In their devotion to a higher cause, they find themselves, most handily, upon a throne."

There came a stiff rapping at the cabin door. "I'm sorry to interrupt, Captain. There is something you must see!"

Skarde rolled off the bed, leaving Sulmei to lounge. He opened the door to Tarsazi. "You interrupt nothing... what is it?"

Tarsazi pointed toward the port side where many men had gathered. Skarde strode to them, and though he was a head taller than all, they opened to give him a place at the rails. Just on the horizon a sail had appeared. The ship was hazy in the distance, but Skarde's keen eyes could just make out its shape.

"That is not one of the Iron Brotherhood's fleet. It's too fat. I'd guess it's a merchant ship," Skarde said.

"Aye," Savo said. "I'd guess we are still in deep waters south of the League-Port towns... perhaps it's trying to avoid detection."

"Or taxes... or pirates," Tarsazi added.

A bolt ran down Skarde's spine, and a smile sprang to his lips. "Well, lads?" Skarde boomed as he turned to face the crew. "Are we vagabonds, or wolves upon the sea?"

"Wolves!" dozens of voices shouted in answer.

"Then set rudder and sail for that juicy morsel, and gather the strongest rowers," Skarde said. "We are slaves no more, but reavers!"

About the Author

Erik lives in a grim and frostbitten kingdom. With a lifetime of passion for fantasy adventure stories he has struck out to forge his own. Besides writing in the little spaces between work, and hanging out with his beloved wife and sprogs, he enjoys heavy metal, playing guitar, medieval history, and weightlifting. He is in it for the sword-swinging thrills.

Other Works by Erik Waag

Samuel Rider: Sword and Seventies
Sword and Seventies: Vol. 1 — That Axe Anciently Was Mine
Sword and Seventies: Vol. 2 — Fangs of the Moon Opal
Sword and Seventies: Vol. 3 — Title T.B.A. (Coming Soon!)

Skarde: The Wandering Sword
Citadel of Seven Swords
Blades Against Fear (Available in Anvil Magazine #2)
Weird of the Skull Totem (First draft complete. Coming Soon!)
Princess of the Shrouded Mountain (Work in progress)

A Humble Request

You, the reader, the enjoyer of sword swinging tales, matter! You, and the community you are a part of, deserve the most satisfying, most action packed, most FUN stories. Please, let me know @WaagBooks on Twitter what you liked, and what you didn't. If you feel I've earned it, please take a moment to RATE and REVIEW my work on Amazon, Goodreads, and elsewhere.

Reviews with comments, even one liners, are powerful and do much to promote indie authors! I would be most grateful to hear from you.

Thank you!

Erik

Printed in Great Britain
by Amazon